S0-BCT-656

WITHDRAWN

SOUTHWEST TALES

SOUTHWEST TALES
A Contemporary Collection

in memory of Tomás Rivera

*edited by Alurista and
Xelina Rojas-Urista*

Maize Press

Maize Press
The Colorado College — Box 10
Colorado Springs, CO 80903

Cover Art by George Cloud

ISBN: 0-939558-09-2
Library of Congress Catalog Card Number: 85-61180

Printed in the United States of America.

Library of Congress Cataloging-in-Publication Data

Southwest tales.

  Bibliography: p.
  1. Short stories, American--Mexican American authors.
2. Short stories, American--Southwestern States.
3. Mexican Americans--Fiction. 4. Southwestern States--
Fiction. 5. American fiction--20th century.
I. Alurista. II. Rojas-Urista, Xelina, 1954-
PS647.M49S68 1986   813'.01'0886872073   85-61180
ISBN 0-939558-09-2

Our memories of Tomás Rivera are filled with joy and respect. This collection is our way of saying thanks for being one to do what needed to be done. A small token of affection for one of the best story tellers in the world of Chicano letters. His work lives on as an example, as a path with heart.

THE EDITORS

CONTENTS

INTRODUCTION

Short fiction has a long, distinguished history in Chicano culture. Just as Anglo-Americans trace their literary antecedents back into English writing, Chicanos can claim prefigurative roots in the Mexican/Latin American/Iberian tradition. This Latino perspective in no way precludes Chicano writers from utilizing their equally legitimate U.S. code, with all it implies. The advantage to having the Latino resource is both its wealth of material — short fiction is perhaps the preferred genre of Latin American writers — and the acceptance that short fiction assumes many forms other than what U.S. academic critics narrowly define as the short story. We need only recall that the ancient Hindu text, *Pañcatantra*, which provided material for many European authors including Shakespeare, entered the Occident, like so much of classical knowledge, through interlingual medieval Spain. The *Pañcatantra's* unknown authors made no distinction between entertaining and teaching: literature was both for pleasure and edification. A jump of several centuries and half the globe into Sixteenth-Century New Mexico finds the tradition flourishing in oral cuentos, which are still heard today, or now read in Chicano stories. Or we could point out innovators like Borjes, Arreola or Monterrosa with their fantastic anecdotes, polished gems of apparently simple, direct statement of the impossible but logical conclusions of reality. Or Octavio Paz's prose poems or Juan Rulfo's descents into the terrifying labyrinths of the human mind. But to continue would be el cuento de nunca acabar, yet another form available to us — but not here.

The point is that Chicanos have a rich tradition of short fiction and our literature reflects this fact. Several books often considered as novels could easily represent short fiction genres. Two of our most respected writers, Tomás Rivera and Rolando Hinojosa, compiled their book-length narratives from a series of stories. Abelardo Delgado garnered the Tonatiuh Prize with an epistolary novel consisting of a series of narratives. Most recently, Sandra Cisneros has won acclaim with *House on Mango Street*, a novelette in Rivera's tradition: a child's development into a budding artist conveyed through a series of related anecdotes. Less known, but equally as deserving of praise, is Sheila Ortiz Taylor's *Faultline*, an excellent novel written in the form of many different voices relating small portions of the whole. And Rudy Anaya, the other Quinto Sol Prize winner, drew heavily on the New Mexican folktale for his novel *Bless Me, Ultima*.

Not that we lack short story writers per se. The first thrust of contemporary Chicano literature produced several now classic stories: Nick C. Vaca's "The Week in the Life," Octavio Romano's "A Rosary for Doña Marina," and Miguel Méndez's "Tata Casehua," were all published in the first anthology of Chicano literature, *El espejo/The Mirror* (1969). That each treated the theme of identity flux in a society where multiethnic values clash to pressure and ultimately destroy the protagonist tells us much about those early writings. Identity in jeopardy, in question, in the fading but not yet reformulated; identity as dilemma, as challenge, as project. Each author played out the question, from the extreme fatalism of Vaca's suicidal professor, to Romano's sexually repressed and selfdestructive Marina, to Méndez's ambiguous absorption of Casehua into the desert sands. Pessimistic content was countered, however, by the mere fact of the story's existence. Chicanos renewed themselves through the word, through the identity of the writer as just that, writer; and through the writer's identity as much more than *just* a writer, but as spokesman for a people. And since the people were not selfdestructing nor disappearing, more optimistic responses followed, specifically from those authors mentioned above. Compare the disintegration of Vaca's professor to the integration found by Rivera's narrator. Significantly the discovery of the narrative process allows Rivera's young man to transcend isolating alienation. Thus Chicano short fiction responds to itself and to the questions raised by the culture outside: thesis-antithesis = synthesis/sin tesis (ojalá) in continual process, a constant working out of possibilities with none the final or definitive version of culture. This is the tradition of polyvalent dynamics within an ever-expanding space of expression into which the narratives of this collection make their appearance.

Each in its way continues the Chicano literary tradition. Kimball and García echo the folktale, with it's final twist of didactic moral. Ramos renders the Llorona myth yet again. Castillo's "The Miracle" treats the community's religious zeal with Fellini-like humor, yet with enough ambiguity to allow for it's possible reality — a sign of respect for tradition as well as good use of irony. Monreal (in "Lola's Return") and Sepúlveda remind me of Romano's regretful retrospection: female characters, trapped in a male-determined world, unjustly lose what they most desire. Ponce's "los tísicos" is similar, yet the discovery of an alternate interpretation of history in the final image places her more in the line of Rivera. Gallego's touching tale easily fits also into the Rivera tradition, yet perhaps closer to Hinojosa in tone and resolution. Treviño's mixture of pop culture and extraneous textual material recalls Oscar Zeta Acosta, though for the surrealistic grotesqueness of Acosta we must go to the fantastic narrative by de la Torre. Both González and Burk create middle class narrators who attempt to comprehend the less privileged; significantly both end by affirming the failure of the attempt (by the characters, not by the text itself): a mixture of nostalgia and a new acceptance of the middle class condition of many authors and a significant number of Chicanos. Monreal's "The Weight Lifters" denounces an oversight in my brief resume of Chicano short fiction: the urban stories of J.L. Navarro.

It is not my intention to lessen the import of these pieces by comparing them to better known ones, but just the opposite. They represent the vitality of the literature in that they continue, expand, restate and reformulate it. To judge them in the context of an anthology would be unfair because it is not each author's own space; only when and if these same authors publish a full collection can we determine their significance with respect to established Chicano writing. I can safely affirm that this collection is highly representative of the themes and approaches found in the literary movement they spring from. Also, it is refreshing to find a collection comprised of so many authors who surely will be new to the average reader. Tomás Rivera could have no more fitting tribute than the publication of these stories, the palpable proof of the continuing extension of the communal word through individual expression.

BRUCE-NOVOA
Trinity University

LOLA'S RETURN

David Nava Monreal

It was a small wedding, the guests consisted of the immediate family and several close friends. The ceremony was performed in the ancient, adobe church on Juarez Street. The priest had unsteady, age mottled hands, a jowl hanging from his chin and a voice that quivered as he recited the matrimonial words. It was early February 1917, the sun shone on the stained-glass windows and they burst with rainbow colors.

Lola wore her mother's old wedding gown. It was made of silk and it shimmered in the warm candlelight. Juan Fuentes, the twenty year old groom, nervously stood next to the bride to be.

Juan was a young fisherman in a Mexican seaside village. He had known Lola since they were children. They played together, gambolled in the same parks, dug for clams in the sand and finally became lovers.

Lola was now eighteen and was considered by many to be the

most beautiful girl in the village. She had fawn-colored hair, translucent brown eyes, light skin, a naturally blushed complexion and a lithe figure that attracted stares. She had waited most of her life to marry Juan. He was kind, industrious and had a handsome way of embarking on a fishing boat. By becoming Juan's wife, Lola felt she could find everlasting happiness.

A tinge of almost imperceptible sadness marred the ceremony. It was the way Lola bent her neck while listening to the priest's word. She knew that as soon as the honeymoon was over, Juan was planning to migrate to the United States. She did not want to go. She loved the fishing village. Mexico. That was where her heart was.

Soon after the rice was tossed, Lola requested that the wedding picture be taken on the white sands of the beach. A tripod was set up and a photograph was taken. She wanted a momento, something to remember the sailboats, gulls and pelicans by.

Juan had ambitions of being a fisherman, of owning his own boat, of making as many American dollars as he could. The first city they entered when they crossed the border was San Diego. Juan was inspired by the ocean and the variety of ships anchored at the docks. He was suffering from an over abundance of optimism. He thought it would be easy to find a job fishing. "I'll start off as a deck hand," he would tell Lola, "work my way up to fisherman, save my money, then buy my own boat."

In time, he found out that things were vastly different.

He could not speak English and make himself understood. He had to find someone to translate for him and even then, he felt himself worlds apart. For various reasons no one would hire him. One crinkled old sailor told him that Mexican seamen got seasick too often, another sailor blatantly said that they could not be trusted. One tall, craggy-faced captain sat him down and explained, "Many a ship is marked because of a Mexican passenger or sailor. There is a revolution going on in your country right now, governments would think you were spying or smuggling guns to Zapata and Villa. I can't afford to be shot out of the ocean because of one Mexican fisherman."

After four months of plodding the wharfs for work, Juan came to realize that he was not wanted in San Diego.

With the twenty dollars they had left, Juan and Lola decided to

2 • David N. Monreal

take a train to the San Joaquin Valley. They had heard there was work there harvesting the fruit that grew on the land. There were even labor camps where they could have housing and the wages were sometimes even as high as fifteen cents an hour.

It was a gloomy afternoon the day they packed. Juan's dream of being a fisherman had crumbled to dust. Lola was grief-stricken as she waited for the train on the wooden bench. What kind of country was this? Where was the gold that lay on the ground like snow? Where were the opportunities, the chances to become rich? It was as savage and cruel as any place they had ever been. Maybe even more. As they boarded the train, Lola was glad she had brought a piece of Mexico with her. The wedding picture in her valise.

Lola looked out the window as the train pulled into the small San Joaquin Valley town. The summer heat was almost unbearable, sun whitened the atmosphere and polished the tree leaves with a lustrous sheen. Lola and Juan stepped off the train, the loose dust settled on their shoes like a fine film of thirst.

By evening they had found a job on a ranch in the outskirts of town. They were given a worker's bungalow reserved for married couples. In reality it was nothing but a dilapidated shack with a bedroom and kitchen. The toilets were outside and they were shared by everyone in the camp.

A spark of happiness came into their lives. Lola lit a fire in the decrepit stove and started making beans and tortillas. Juan watched her, for the first time in a long while he was smiling. This was what he was searching for, the kind of life he dreamt of; Lola in a light-colored dress with her hair tied in a bun, smelling sweet and womanly. A flame reflected off her pretty face, Juan saw a future come into focus.

A day later they were in the fields, harvesting the plums. The work was hot and dirty, the sun relentlessly beat down on their brows. They had never done this kind of work before. They struggled with the huge wooden ladders, dragging them from tree to tree. The humid heat inside the tangled limbs sapped them of their energy and strength. Gnats and wasps constantly buzzed around their heads, dust from the leaves flew into their eyes — Lola's hands were scratched by the broken branches and Juan was bitten by a spider on the back of the neck.

For a month they continued the strenuous work. Getting up at five in the morning and leaving the fields at six in the evening. Six days a week they worked. One day Lola was standing on the last rung of the ladder, reaching for a solitary plum, when she toppled and fell to the ground, hip first. She let out a painful wail. Grabbing at her stomach she began to cry. Juan held her hand as she writhed on the ground, she held her belly as though she were about to die. At last, after she was calmed down by her husband's soothing words, she said, "What if I killed him?"

She had not told Juan that she was pregnant.

Lola spent the night in excruciating pain. She lay next to Juan weeping into the early morning hours. Juan did everything he could for her; he put cold towels on her forehead to reduce the fever. When the foreman came by with the truck to pick them up for work, Juan explained that his wife was terribly sick and needed a doctor. "We haven't any doctors available here," the burly man exclaimed. "Besides, the field has to be finished by the end of the month. We need your wife to work."

"But she is seec." Juan replied in his broken English.

"I don't give a god damn! Either she comes to work or you two can move out of here!"

By the time Juan ran back into the house Lola was standing up putting on her work clothes. "You don't have to go," Juan said.

Tying the red bandana over her head, she replied, "I'll be alright, Juan. Don't worry."

Lola worked through the rest of the summer. By the end of September she was far into her sixth month of pregnancy. After the plums had been harvested, the olives needed to be picked. Ignoring Juan's protests, she continued to work side by side with her husband.

One night, in the middle of December, Lola started having labor pains. They were stronger than most women's and she had to bite down on a leather belt to keep from screaming. Juan called a neighborhood woman to help him with the birth. They stayed with Lola through the night. Juan sat in the kitchen, drinking a beer, listening to Lola's whimpers and moans. At last, after what seemed like days of agony, an old woman walked out of the bedroom and announced the news to Juan. "You have a son." She said.

"A son?" Juan repeated, almost crying.

"But he has been born deformed and Lola will not be able to have another child."

This time, Juan did cry.

Juanito was born a Mongolian idiot and the fingers of both his

4 • David N. Monreal

hands were pasted together like duck's feet. As a three year old boy he would slobber on his clothes and lick the food off the floor. Lola loved him more than she had loved anything in her entire life. She would take him to the "fields" with her and breast feed him under the quiet shadows of the walnut trees. Sometimes she would carry him to the reed scattered irrigation ditch and show him the croaking frogs as she tickled his nose with a dandelion. He would emit a gurgling laugh and clumsily clap his gnarled hands with joy. The older he grew the more apparent it became that he would live his life in pathetic retardation.

When Juanito turned seven his father began using him as a symbol of his failing life. Whenever Juan's friends would come to the house, he would point to his cretin son playing on the porch and say, "You see what this country has done for me. Given me an idiot for a son."

"Then why don't you go back to Mexico?" Some men would ask.

Sadly, Juan could only answer, "There would be more shame waiting for me there."

Lola began to worry when Juan started calling Juanito vile names. She could not understand how a father could hate his own child. At the dinner table she could see his eyes light up with hatred whenever he was to look at Juanito. The bitterness Juan felt was not meant to be directed toward the innocent boy, but at himself. After ten years things did not work out the way he had planned them. He had wanted more from life, he had hoped for a strong, normal son, instead they lived in poverty, his wife had been made barren, his ambition of owning a fishing boat had all but vanished. Even Lola was silently suffering within herself. She missed her friends and family, and she still had the strong urge to go back to Mexico.

For two years the Fuentes family lived in relative contentment. The children in the neighborhood had gotten used to Juanito as a kind of "village idiot". There were days when the kids would come visit and play with him as though he was as normal as anyone else. Even Juan started to pay more attention to him. Several times he took him to the river to fish for trout. On another occasion he accompanied him to the neighborhood baseball game. If there was jeering or snickering it was being done by the people that knew nothing of Juanito's gentleness.

In the summer of 1930, Lola was visited by a woman who worked for the 'Rehabilitation Services'. She was a tall, gaunt young girl suited in a dark dress down to her ankles, accentuating her shapeless body.

She sat Lola down and gave her a thorough explanation, "Juanito must start attending school. It isn't fair for him to spend his life uneducated. What will he do once you and your husband are gone? We have these new methods that work wonders on people like Juanito."

Lola could not comprehend everything told to her, but she could sense they wanted to take Juanito away. "But he is happy here." Lola tried explaining.

"It's a state law, ma'am." The girl said, pursing her red lips. "Your son is sick. He can't be allowed to run about the streets without any kind of training."

Lola turned her face away in sorrow, "I don't like to break laws," she said.

Four years later, when Juanito was sixteen, Miss Wallace, the teacher at the school, phoned Lola. "Mrs. Fuentes," she said, "This is a big day for your son, Juanito."

"What do you mean?" Lola asked.

"Instead of taking the bus, he is going to walk home."

"No, no! Don't let him do that!" Her heart fluttered with anxiety. "He's afraid. He will hurt himself!"

"Calm yourself, Mrs. Fuentes." Said the confident teacher. "This will be the best thing for him. He needs to be independent. He has to do things on his own."

"His father will be home in an hour. He will go pick him up," Lola said desperately.

"No." Miss Wallace sternly raised her voice. "This is for his own good. Now good-bye."

Lola hung up and paced the floor. This was not right. It was not fair for someone to dictate to her child; this was another of the white man's schemes to destroy the Mexican.

Lola ran up and down the house nervously pulling at her hair. She could imagine her helpless, confused son meandering through the streets. What if he got hit by a car? She would never forgive Miss Wallace or that damn school! And the dogs, how about the dogs? There were many wild and dangerous beasts roaming around free!

Thirty minutes went by, then an hour. Lola stood at the window every second. She was praying to God that nothing happened to Juanito. Maybe Juan would drive in and go out looking for him, he should be home any time now. Lola got restless and went out to the front gate. She looked down the street for any sign of Juanito. Sud-

6 • David N. Monreal

denly a car, ornamented in chrome and shining accessories, turned the corner at a high speed. She strained her eyes and could see that all the passengers were white and youthful. They were driving directly at her; Lola stepped off the curb and got back into her yard. The car slowed down, then stopped in front of the gate. The back door opened and one of the boys spoke in a shrill voice, "We thought this crazy spic needed a ride." And from the back of the car, rolled Juanito, battered and bloodied, with his eyes closed and his face covered with dirt. The car sped away as the body hit the ground. Lola screamed as though she meant to wake up the world.

The doctor diagnosed the cause of Juanito's death as massive internal bleeding. He had been beaten all over the body with clubs and fists. There were several knife wounds on his forearms and one just below his pectoral muscle. Most of the barrio attended the wake. He looked almost angelic in his velvet lined casket, his face showed no signs of being beaten and on his thin, boyish lips was a subtle mischievous smile; almost like the smile spread on his face when he played among a crowd of romping, happy children.

The police scoured the city for Juanito's assailants. It took them over a month to round up four suspects. Lola was called in to the police station to identify the four teenagers. The moment she saw them she let out a scream, "Yes! Those are the ones who killed my Juanito!" It took almost three more months to organize a trial, the defense lawyers kept appealing the case, asking for more time to contact witnesses. The prosecution did almost nothing. The only thing they did to build up their case, was ask Lola to describe what she saw in detail. She told them the same story over five times.

In the courtroom Lola was asked to testify, she sat on the witness chair in tears, pointing at the defendants. "Those are the boys I saw in the car. They pulled up to the front gate and threw Juanito's body out of the backseat. They were laughing and insulting Juanito's nationality." She sobbed, for it was a pain to look into their faces, "Someday they will burn in hell!"

One of the defense lawyers approached her with a question, "Isn't it true Mrs. Fuentes that you are required to wear eyeglasses at all times?"

"Yes." She replied, vaguely aware of her answer.

"Were you wearing them the time you said you saw these four

boys in the car?", the lawyer asked dramatically pointing at the defendants.

"I can't remember." She answered.

"Well, we can Mrs. Fuentes. In our investigations we discovered that you had broken your glasses the day before and they were in the optometrist's office being repaired. And we further questioned your optometrist and discovered that you cannot see ten feet in front of your face without them. In light of this, Mrs. Fuentes, can you explain how you can positively identify these boys when you were not wearing your glasses?"

Lola was bewildered as she gazed across the courtroom. She glanced toward Juan and saw the blank look of fear on his face. Her voice quivered as she spoke, "I just know."

It did not take long for the charges to be dropped on the four boys. There was a lack of evidence. No one saw them do anything. And if there was someone, they would never come forward.

Lola and Juan mourned the results of the trial. They had not been avenged. At home, in a torrent of tears, Lola wailed, "Is this justice?"

As the years passed the loss of Juanito left the Fuentes' with a scar of emptiness that never healed. Lola seemed to have grown old overnight. Her hair turned gray, the face that was once burnished by youth now was seamed and eroded by sorrow. She grew listless. She kept to herself, she rarely conversed with the neighbors like she used to and her laughter that echoed through the house was heard no more.

Juan was the one damaged the most. He suffered his misery inwardly, quietly letting it eat away at his spirit. He took to drinking and staying out late at night; a day never went by that he did not consume two or three pints of whiskey. Lola made a feeble attempt to help him, but she had her own pain to grapple with. He would stumble home in a drunken stupor, cursing at the top of his voice, "What have I done to my life? What happened to me, Juanito!"

Lola could sympathize with his laments. If they had only stayed at home. But instead of saying anything she would lie next to him on the bed and try to sleep under the stench of his liquor doused body.

One night as Lola lay in her bed sleeping, there was some pounding at the door. She got up, put on her housecoat and answered it. Standing outside the threshold was an old man nervously twisting a soiled hat in his hands. "Mrs. Fuentes." He said in a somber voice. "I have some bad news for you. I don't know how to say it without causing you pain, but your husband died of a heart attack tonight."

The old man was surprised by Lola's calm. "Where did it happen?" She asked.

"Down at the cantina. He was drinking . . ."

Putting up her hand to hush him, she said, "I know, it was bound to happen someday. He drank too much." Pausing she added, "Where is he now?"

"In the morgue," answered the wrinkled man.

"Let me get dressed and I'll go with you."

As Lola put on her clothes she made a light rustling sound. The dim lightbulbs palely illuminated the dingy walls in her bedroom. She did not feel like weeping or sobbing. She felt nothing. She was disturbed that she could be so numb at a time like this. She forcibly tried to cry, but all her emotions seemed to have been drained, completely disintegrated. With grace she went with the old man to the morgue, the first step into the midnight air made her realize that she had been left alone at fifty.

Lola slowly began to grow her garden. In her empty hours she would till the soil and plant a new seed. As the shrubbery and flowers grew tall around her house, a sense of well being entered her. She felt secure, hidden from the world that had hurt her so much. As the years passed she seeded trees that darkened her roof with shade. She implanted ivy that entwined in her fence and kept her obscured from prying eyes. Along her southern wall tall sunflowers swayed and dipped in the breeze. On the northern end of her house huge bamboo shoots grew, creaking in the high winds. In the front yard a grove of pomegranate trees flourished, infested constantly by an army of flitting hummingbirds. In time, after decades of vigorous gardening, Lola had surrounded herself by a kind of vegetable sanctuary.

She was being seen by neighbors less and less. She had no reason to go shopping; she made her own clothes, grew her own food, the chickens that scratched in her yard provided her with eggs and poultry. She wore plain cotton dresses and kept her long hair enwrapped in a black rebozo. The only sound she made, the only proof of her existence was the cracking of dry leaves as she walked through her monastic maze.

In the silence of her home she wept and yearned for Mexico. She wrote letters to her fishing village, addressing them to forgotten friends. She waited months upon months for an answer, but nothing came. She had visions as she worked in her garden. She saw the great fishing yachts sketched against the blue sky. She heard the gulls shrieking and saw the silhouette of a pelican pass over the sun. As she watered her sagging roses she felt the ocean fill her nostrils with its salty scent. She heard the splashing of waves, the pounding of horses, the sweet voice of her mother. Meanwhile, the earth outside was permeated with bitterness and cruelty. People were cheating, hurting each other. America was raving mad. She felt pity for the changing world.

In moments of deep aloneness Lola would take out her wedding picture and touch it to her cheek. The mystery of Mexico would come back to her as though seeping through her flesh. She heard music, laughter, and felt a surge of happiness that could not be denied. At the age of seventy-seven she died quietly in her bed of tuberculosis. But she defeated them all, before she passed away, she returned to her beloved country by pressing the old photograph to her heart.

TATA FINO

Francisca H. Tenorio

I remember when I was little, viendo una foto que tenía mi mamá de Tata Fino quebrando un potrillo alazán. El y el potrillo eran uno con el viento. He was flying in the air . . . holding the mane con una mano fuerte y su sombrero con la otra. (Eat your heart out Cisco.) Caballero como él no había. Venian por él desde ranchos lejos en la sierra sus primos y amigos para que él les quiebrara sus broncos. No había quien le ganara con los caballos. Era jinete through and through.

Pues pasaron los años. Zarafino y Modesta had six children. Two died of illness de niños. Mi abuelita . . . culeca con sus hijos. She wrapped her life around her children y su religión. Sus rezos, dirigía a los santos y martires . . . martyrs like herself. No tenía descanso esa mujer.

She took good care of Tata Fino in motherly ways rather than as the passionate lover he had begged her so strongly to be en esos años pasados . . . the lover she had refused to be until he stopped pursuing the dream of passion between them. Ella se la pasaba trabajando o en rodillas con el silencio y su tristeza.

No era llorona la Modesta. She was a powerful woman. Fuerte como las raizes del álamo outside their house. De buenas a primeras se le antojaba a Modesta to build a room y lo hacía. She built all the rooms onto the house con la ayuda de sus hijos y vecinas. Ella hizo los adobes with her hands . . . the same hands with which she tended her three acre garden every year y su familia every day, con esas mismas manos, Modesta acariciaba su rosario cada noche as she prayed delante del crucifijo por su familia. Oh, she was a tiny woman, only four feet, ten inches short but she was heavy duty competition for most any man. Fuerte como una mula, era decidida. . . aguantadora.

Tata Fino la apreciaba. With time he could see Modesta's expression of love. Agradecía a su esposa, her virtues and beliefs . . . agradecía que era buena mamá. Her family was her total life.

Tata was never un borracho pero le pegaba a la botella de vez en cuando . . . (like every day.) Al hacer eso, nunca acababa borracho. El licor solo le soltaba mas el alma. He always was a good provider for his family. Cuidaba y amaba mucho a sus hijos y hijitas.

With the years grandma grew to spill her troubles to her vecinas, comadres y familia. "Tu papá es un borracho," she'd yell out at her children when he was outside playing the guitar and singing the night away. With time y poco juicio, her children disregarded many of her complaints about their papá. "No es borracho mi papá." Lo defendían dándole contra a su mamá. Ella les respondía . . . "Ah, de noche todos los gatos son pardos. ¿Qué saben ustedes?"

Pues his children defended him. He was their papá y lo respetaban y además they loved him solo por su modo de ser. My Tata always took care of his familia y aunque le gustaba la vida muy movida, no era capaz de descuidarse de sus hijos. Les enseño a tocar la guitarra and he shared with them his love for horses. The affection he had for his children nourished the love between them. El nunca salía a la calle to drag his family into mitotes.

Well, with time, the inevitable happened. I never knew how Grandma found out . . . sería por el pinche mitote que destroza vidas y familias. At any rate, Tata Fino had a lover.

Antes de meter un píe en la sepultura . . . despúes de tanto año

14 • Francisca H. Tenorio

fanning the flame of passion that burned in him all through his youthful years. Ahora con las canas de los años que robaron su madurez y dejaron la copa de su vida llena de experencias . . . ahora Zarafino bebió un brindis al gusto de saber que it wasn't a dream . . . she did exist. Su nombre . . . Andrea. "Andrea, mi estrella," le decía Fino with a smile. Ella le respondía, "Fino, mi destino." They'd laugh and cry together, siempre con pasión.

Ay, Tata. En la tela del querer que tenían uno por el otro, you found a binding love with unrestrained pleasure, pain and ecstasy. Your need for Andrea drove you both to the brink of madness. In each other you found the partner of your dreams. Fate had it que sus veredas se cruzaran. She was la hembra que deseabas todos esos años. La tigresa que te escarbó la pasión de tu juventud, bringing your raw soul to the surface with her intensity, her wild laughter y sus miradas que te encendían. She soaked up the passion that spilled de tus entrañas. Ella te deseó . . . ella se perdió en tus besos y ternura. Ella te conoció as no one ever did.

La familia nunca supo how long you had been seeing her, Tata. ¿Cuánto tiempo habían pasado bebiendo el vino del amor . . . juntos . . . peleándole al tiempo which robbed you of minutes, hours and years together? All we knew was you were both driven to keep seeing each other even after Grandma knew.

Mi mamá le platicaba a la vecina about the scene when Grandma Modesta supo de "la cosa" . . . as she later called it.

Esa noche, pensando que ya estaba la familia dormida, mi abuelita se quitó el delantal and she layed it on the table donde estaba sentada en silencio tomando una taza de café con Tata Fino, late at night. "Zarafino, si no hay nada mas entre nosotros después de tantos años juntos, espero que siquiera exista la verdad. Dime si és o no és. ¿Qué existe una cosa entre tu y la Andrea?"

Tata volteo a verla. En sus ojos vió el mero diablo de esos años pasados . . . la endemoniada de aquella noche de rabia cuando le había dicho Modesta que ella quería su pasión solo para darle hijos. Esta vez Tata had no words. Ya para él las palabras salían sobrando. Hay cosas que se dicen sin hablar. He looked into her eyes sensing her pain. "Sí Modesta, sí es verdad."

¡Pucha! Modesta vomitó en renegos el enfado que le envenenaba la sangre. "¡Infiel! ¡Condenado! Yo cuidándote y a tu familia todos estos años y así me pagas . . . desgraciado . . . ¡PUTO! ¿Qué no piensas en tu familia? Ya te volviste completamente loco." As her rage grew so did her desperation. "¿Qué haces tras de la hermosura de esa caprichosa a tu edad? Ya tus hijos son adolecentes y tu todavía de esa misma edad. Es que esa mujer te ha vuelto loco. Te ha engañado. Te ha confundido. Yo conozco a su familia. Es de los mismos Chavez que la Victoriana. Decían que la Victoriana ere bruja. Andrea es su nieta . . . ella también será bruja. Te embrujó. ¡Confiésate! ¡Arrepiéntete! ¡Condenado!"

De manera que el mitote se volvió un lío. Modesta couldn't deal with this pain. She was truly shattered. Groping for hope, le dijo a toda la familia de su papá. La bronca no tenía pies ni cabeza. El enredo fue creciendo. It grew more complicated for everyone concerned hasta que todo se volvió un nudo. It wasn't a clear cut situation. De todos lados creció "la cosa". Everyone knew que Tata was still seeing Andrea . . . their love . . . as powerful as ever.

Grandma Modesta really didn't want to accept the fact that Fino had found the one partner who fulfilled him. She looked to her coma-dre, Clara, for a shred of support, trying to keep her cool, although she sat con los pedazos de su vida en sus manos. With disgust, le dijo Modesta a la Clara, trying to convince herself, "Ahh, ya cuando los hombres miran que se quedan viejos, buscan una graciosa jovencita con quien probar que todavía son machos. Ya Fino perdió la mente. Yo ni me pongo a gastar mis celos en ese borracho y menos en esa puta. El que le lava la cara al burro pierde su tiempo y pierde el jabón. Que se vayan al diasque los dos. ¿Qué me importa a mí?"

Clara knew the facts and was up front . . . that's why Grandma chose to talk with her. Tanto como knowing the truth hurt Modesta, el dolor de saber aroused her sensually in a bizarre manner. Listening to Clara's details de la pasión entre Fino y Andrea fascinated Modesta. She took in every painful word Clara said describing "la cosa."

Clara sat quietly and slowly rolled a cigarette. Hechó el saquito de tabaco en la bolsa de su delantal and she looked into Modesta's eager eyes as she lit the cigarette. Clara le dijo, "No Modesta. Fino no perdió la mente. Muchas son las mujeres de Rincón que le dieran todo a tu Fino al decirles él una sola palabra. Es hombre que les saca el deseo a las mujeres solo con la fuerza de su carácter. Atrae atención él sin ningún esfuerzo. No. Yo te diré, Modesta . . . ahora Fino esta compen-sando por una perdida . . . por tantos años que no le hiciste caso. En todos aquellos años fue contigo que quería repartir esa pasión tan

16 • Francisca H. Tenorio

fuerte que sentía. Milagro que no se halló otra Andrea antes de esto. Es que él no salía a buscar mujer. El supo que si tenía que ser . . . el no tenía que buscar. Ella llegaría a su lado . . . y así fue la cosa. Así es Zarafino. Por eso lo desean tantas. Es hombre Fino. Hombre que brilla entre los muchachos, entre los hombres de su edad. No es viejo, Modesta. No te equivoques. Está gozando del medio día de su vida. Tu, la loca que lo tenías en la madrugada de sus años . . . tu que no lo apreciabas."

Siguieron juntos muchos años, Tata Fino y Andrea hasta ese día del otoño. Esa tarde nublosa Fino y Andrea se paseaban juntos en el caballo favorito de Andrea . . . un caballo ballo . . . a beautiful animal whose wild, unpredictable nature thrilled his riders . . . Tata y su Estrella. Ese día montaron el caballo al pelo, Andrea holding Tata's waist as the unrestrained steed carried the two free souls into the brewing October storm. Esa tarde el cielo estaba vestido de luto . . . enojado y místico. You could smell the rainclouds ready to explode. The rumble could be felt stirring in the sky. Con la fuerza de los dioses se soltaron truenos y centellas. Tata raced the stallion against time and the impending storm towards the corral . . . sensing the danger only too clearly . . . Andrea con confianza y su pelo volando en el viento.

Sería un trueno, lo que espantó al caballo ballo ese día obscuro de octubre. Respingó de repente y cayó Andrea aunque Tata grabbed for her in vain. A broken neck took her from him in that unchangeable instant of their destiny.

Los llantos de Tata siguieron día y noche. Quiet tears, he shared with no one . . . lagrimas he cried inside his soul. He mourned Andrea con la misma pasión con que la amó todos esos años. He called her in his sleep. Caiban sus llantos hasta el suelo de su corazón . . . su corazón tan vacío ahora with his loss. La botella was the lover who replaced a su Estrella. Se apartó de todos. He would spend hours alone perdido en el trago . . . the liquor which stirred the guilt he felt at not having saved Andrea . . . por su pura pendejada of suggesting a daring ride on that stormy day. Why hadn't he used his common sense? Sus pensamientos revived the memories of the reckless love and daring with which he and Andrea faced life together. "Aiii . . . muerte . . . ¿porqué mi Andrea?" preguntaba solo en su borrachera, solo arrastrándose en su tristeza. "Porqué no fuí yo él que murió? ¿Qué vale mi vida ya sin ella?"

Unos meses después del acidente llegó la comadre Clara a visitar. "Ah, Modesta" le dijo con suspiro, "Que día tan hermoso. El primer día de la primavera." Modesta grew more and more relieved in time by Clara's healing visits. She was having a very hard time dealing with Zarafino's drinking and grief at his loss of Andrea. Modesta reached out to Clara, soltando su agrura. "Qué entras tú cantando de la primavera. Para mí solo me sirve saber que ya es primavera como recuerdo que pasó todo el invierno borracho Zarafino. Lo embrujó esa Andrea. ¿Irá a seguir bebiendo hasta que caiga muerto? ¿Irá a seguir tirado por los suelos con sus amargos llantos y fiel tristeza por ese bruja? ¡Ave María Purísima! Por qué fue a entrar a nuestras vidas esa hechizera? Porqué este castigo? Fino no habla ya con nadie desde el accidente. Nunca me hablaba mucho antes, pero ahora, peor queda de un dia pa'l otro. Ya no sale de su cuarto. Mas valiera que se muriera."

Clara listened intently as she traced the red and white pattern on the plastic tablecloth, sensing her comadre's cry for help and knowing all too well that Modesta couldn't live with the pain of realizing daily that Fino could have that much love inside him . . . all that love she had rejected years ago. Clara looked into Modesta's eyes. "Modesta, yo quiero hablar con Fino." Modesta was relieved. She had always valued Clara's words . . . the way she had of bringing things into focus. If anyone could help Fino, she knew that it was Clara. Zarafino respetaba a la Clara.

Reaching the back end of the house, Clara tocó la puerta to the cuartito where Fino lay tendido con una botella, su inconsolable tristeza and his bitter guilt. "Soy yo, Clara, ¿Puedo entrar?"

Fino couldn't tell her "No." Something about Clara attracted him. He saw alot of himself in her eyes. He didn't answer her second knock but felt relief when Clara entered, slowly closing the door behind her, standing against the door, her hand deep in her apron pocket. She asked, "¿Me puedo sentar en la cama, Fino?" He sat up in the bed where he lay in rumpled clothes he hadn't changed for days. Clara sat on the squeaky bed, sacó su saquito de tabaco y rolló un cigarrito. Le pasó el tabaco a Fino and he rolled himself one too. Sacó una mecha, la rayó con su uña y le prendió el cigarrito a Clara after lighting his.

"¿Te has visto en un espejo este invierno Fino?" Clara asked as she inhaled her cigarette, squinting her reaching eyes. Silence followed her words hasta que Clara acabó con su cigarro, holding the bacha to her lips with her thumb and forefinger to savor the last remaining smoke.

She looked deeply into Fino's eyes. "De la suerte, Fino, y de la muerte, no hay quien se escape. Ya era su tiempo. Ya por todo lo que la hubieras querido salvar, no hubieras podido hacer nada. La muerte no tiene corazón . . . solo una mano helada que nos deja saber sin palabras que ya llegó la hora. Por muy fuerte que seas Fino, no pudieras haber peleado con la muerte si ya estaba decidida. Nadie, Fino, ni tú ni yo. Yo le quize pelear muchos años pasados cuando se llevó al gran amor de mi vida pero aprendí con los años que es inútil . . . después de pasar años así como estás tú ahora. Aprendí con el tiempo. El tiempo cura al enfermo, no el ungüento que le embarran. Tu no te moriste, Fino . . . anque quizieras. Todavía te arde muy fuerte la vida por dentro. Cuando te llege la hora . . . te irás. No Fino, estas vivo. Sal a pelearle a la vida y a gozar del tiempo que te falta. Es una perdida para todos nosotros los vivos, no tenerte. Si te hubieras muerto fuera otra cosa pero no estás muerto, Fino. Queremos seguir gozando de tu inspiración. Te necesitamos nosotros los que seguimos este pinche camino chingón de la vida. Soy egoista, Fino. Me enojo al saber que estás tirando tus horas contra las paredes de este cuartito cuando te necesitamos tanto."

She picked up his guitarra from the corner of the room. Le limpió el polvo con sus dedos and she strummed the strings slowly as she sat on the bed with only thoughts and no words. Después de mucho silencio she looked at Fino and put her hand on his, transmitiendo su remedio de cariño y interés. She lay the guitar on the bed and rolled another cigarette. Fumaron en el silencio por mucho tiempo. Mudo, Fino reached for Clara's hand y con ternura he leaned forward to kiss her weathered fingers. She stood slowly, reaching down for his head. She pressed it firmly into her apron . . . into the pulsating rhythm of her soul. She buried both her hands in the thick crispness of his tangled hair and pressed him against her womb. She held him like this with all her being and he knew then . . . he was alive. They treasured the moment. The respect between them didn't interfere with their silent messages to each other. Tomando ella un resuello tembloroso que luchaba con sus pulmones, Clara's vibrant hands caressed his hair, his face and neck. She knelt and looked deep into his eyes. They said it all sin mas palabras. Fino smiled faintly, looking at the floor. Clara lo besó en la frente y se paró.

Picking up the guitarra y dándosela a Fino, le dijo . . . "Ya basta de tanta tristeza Fino. Cosas entran a nuestras vidas y así también con el tiempo cosas salen. Entra otra vez a las vidas de los que te necesitan . . . los que te quieren. Te necesitamos este fin de semana, Fino.

Queremos que cantes en la fiesta que vamos a tener para darle la bienvenida a la primavera. Toma . . . practica y allá te veo este sábado. Llega temprano porque vamos a azar unos dos cabritos."

Well, Fino was there Saturday night. Ese día dió gracias por la primavera que llegó y por la vida que le volvió. Siguió por muchos años Tata Fino . . . animado as in his days of youth pero acumulando experiencias en la copa de su vida . . . experiences which made him Zarafino. Parecía que el tiempo no le robaba la juventud del alma a Tata. Cantaba con todo el mundo . . . his songs more overwhelming than ever for the richness of his life. Cantaba de alegría con la misma pasión que cantaba de la vida y muerte trágica en sus corridos. Aunque time robbed his body of it's youth, siguió fuerte como siempre. . . breaking horses y paseándose por su querida tierra.

Time played a dirty trick on Tata, though. Con los años comenzó a perder su vista. El doctor no le hayó remedio. At first he refused to believe it pero entre más tiempo, más iba quendando a obscuras. En unos años se dió cuenta que lo esperaba el destino de ser incapaz de seguir su vida como siempre. Ya casi no hallaba la vereda al corral. Con tiempo ya no pudo ni pasearse a caballo.

Tata no supo how to deal with this blow to his vitality. Todo empezó a cambiar and Tata went downhill. He had to be led around como un niño. En su temor he grabbed for his pride and sanity. No se dejó caer por los suelos . . . to be treated as an invalid.

No se dejaba dar lástima. He knew that it was hopeless if he totally despaired in himself . . . if he gave up and lost his will. In spite of his struggle to fight it, however, his depression grew. It began to conquer him. He hardly cared for himself anymore . . . solo en lo más esencial.

Grandma tried to convince the family. "Yo sé que esa hechizera lo embrujó. Lo hizo perder su mente en aquellos años y ahora está perdiendo su vista y salud. Los doctores no saben que hacer. Antes de que quede en un asilo lo vamos a tener que llevar a alguien que le ayude, como una curandera, si . . . una curandera. Lo llevaremos a ver a la Margarita. Si alguien le puede ayudar es ella. Lo llevamos antes de que quede bien ciego y loco."

Tata refused to go at first pero todavía tenía the faintest ray of hope that something could change his destiny of being blind. He finally agreed y fue a visitar a la Margarita . . . rogando por la limosna de que lo curara.

Los remedios de la curandera no le ayudaron. Siguió perdiendo más y más la vista. Los consejos de la Margarita . . . he didn't want. He became obsessed with the desire to regain his eyesight pero entre más tiempo . . . peor quedó, hasta que en fin no pudo ver nada . . . ni las telarañas de luz. He was totally blind.

In his pride insistía en hacer todo por sí mismo. It hurt his family to see his decline. His stubborn efforts of will to maintain his independence often met with more failures than successes. Se le caian cosas. . . tropezaba. He was often forced to accept help. Cuando se descuidaba su familia, salía, pa' fuera solo a usar el escusado. Su orgullo no lo dejaba usar el basín como niño. Allá lo hallaba su familia tangled in barbed wire fences o en las cizañas ensangrentado . . . cortado y con moretones por los trancazos que se daba el pobre Tata. The worst injuries he was suffering though, were the inner doubts which were killing his sense of hope. En esos años cortos, he lived a dark eternity. No pudo vivir con ese castigo.

Sería the ardent struggle of life and death within him que se lo llevó al fin.

Fue en enero de un invierno helado y nevoso. La nieve había comensado fuerte a las cuartro de la tarde. Mi tio Julián había salido a echarles comida a los animales cuando fue notando que la puerta del corral estaba abierta de par en par. El caballo favorito de Tata Fino se había salido. Lo buscó pero the snow had covered his tracks completely.

Tio Julián went in the house where Tata y Modesta sat at the table tomando un cafecito. "Ya ese caballo loco de usted se salió del corral otra vez Tata, pero ahora no lo veo por la nieve." Modesta sprang up in quick response. "Pues que se vaya ese caballo condenado. Tiene mala maña. No es mansito, sinó, cree que debe de estar suelto. Está bronco. Que se vaya . . . ¿quién diablos va a salir a buscarlo con esta nevada?"

Tata stood up enfurecido. "Vamos Julián. Me llevas a buscarlo. Ese caballo me vale el oro solo por su ánimo . . . porque me pelea y no se deja amansar." Tata put his jacket on but Julián refused to take him. "Ya lo busqué Tata. Se salió antes de que comenzara a nevar porque no hay rastros. Hay mucha nieve. No se puede ver. Hay lo haya un vecino. Ya saben de quién es ese caballo moro, mostrenco y loco."

Peleó y averiguó Tata. "¿Qué saben ustedes de caballos? Saben cuatro letras y están a obscuras. Yo lo hayo hasta sin mis ojos. Si no quieren ir, voy solo," les gritaba. "Yo conozco ese caballo moro ya después de tantos años de estar juntos. Solo yo le sé."

Grandma Modesta le gritó perdiendo su paciencia after an hour of insane arguments. "No vás y se acabó el pleito. Ya estás perdiendo la mente de vuelta. Ya cállate y déjate de estas locuras."

Enrabiado, Tata threw his jacket on the floor y se fúe a su cuarto. Tropezó donde iba con una muñeca que había dejado su nietecita en el suelo. Renegó hasta que llegó a su cuarto pero se sosiegó . . . or at least so the family thought.

A la media noche cuando ya estaban todos bien dormidos, de terco y arriesgado, salió en la nieve en busca de su caballo moro. His determination carried him over the deep snow banks into holes and into trees pero siguió . . . decidido y guiado por la lumbre de su firmeza. He felt the fire and once again he knew he was alive.

A las seis de la mañanita cuando despertó Modesta, sintió que algo no estaba bién. Entró a la cocina a hechar lumbre pa' el café cuando vio que la chaqueta de Tata no estaba. Sacudió a mi tio Julián to wake him in her panic. Los dos corrieron al corral. Tata's footprints traced a clearcut path in the deep, fresh snow.

In desperation, Julián ran, dejando a Modesta con su temor, al ladito del corral. Julián corrió por media hora en la lucecita de la luna which reflected on the snow esa madrugada. Allá, a lo lejos veo dos figuras que apenas se podian distingir. "¡Tata!" gritaba Tio Julián, unable to catch his breath for panic and exhaustion. "Tata," as he approached the distant figures. He recognized Tata walking con su caballo perdido a su lado. Fino's clothes and hair were soaking wet . . . a look of satisfaction and exhaustion of his face.

Se tardó cinco días la pulmonia en llevárselo. Hasta sin querer . . . le seguía ardiendo la lumbre . . . la pasión de su vida. As he lay in un delirio in his final hours . . . llamaba a Andrea. Murió en los brazos de su familia . . . su esposa a su lado.

Clara lo veló también y esa noche que murió Tata, she was a comfort to the living at his bedside. Ya que cobijaron su cuerpo . . . vacio de vida, con la sábana . . . Modesta cried in Clara's arms. "¿Porqué? Dime Clara. ¿Porqué? Por Dios santo dime ¿Porqué?" Clara stood in silence holding her comadre, drowning Modesta's uncontrollable sobs in her breast. Al fin Clara respondió tranquilamente, "Porque así tenía que ser, Modesta. Porque así fue todo."

THE HARVEST

Julian S. Garcia

The cold air hangs in the predawn light. The old people bundle their heads and wrap heavy ponchos on their shoulders. They run out to the fields with their shadows behind them. They grunt and moan and their feet sink into the black soil. Some use bristled brooms to sweep dirt from their shacks. On the porch there are coffee cans protecting their Begonias.

Mago sat drinking his whisky-laden coffee and watched them from the enclosed screen of his porch. He had a tarp sheet over his menagerie of plants. He was the only man in Refugio who had Salvadorean peasants working for him.

"*Trabajen mas!*" he bellowed.

The old people shuffled their feet like old mules. He smiled and then swallowed the remains of his coffee. He made a sweeping gesture and two women appeared from his bricked home. They were not his daughters. Mago was not married.

"*Gracias*, Elena," he said to one of them.

The two were half his age. One barely eighteen, the other just twenty-five. Elena was short, her hips curved like a pear and her breasts pointy, firm. She had glossy white teeth and her toasted body glistened like morning dew. The other had porcelain skin; her emerald eyes like a cat's.

"A kiss mi *prieta*," Mago laughed. Maria bent down to kiss him, and Mago ran his finger underneath her skirt. He wiggled his finger along her hard buttocks. "*Pendeja*," Elena giggled as she ran back into the house.

Mago peered out to the gravel road which had been imprinted with tire tracks and boot indentions. Beyond the road was a *monte* full of wild creatures. He had not slipped into the forest since the death of his grandfather who still lingered in his heart unlike the peasants whom he felt no compassion for. From afar, he would hear faint cries of pigs being slaughtered and then the bitter smell of dead animals.

At the end of the day, the peasants returned from the fields. One of them had a strongbox.

"What now Gonzales?" Mago asked.

"We have found this box."

"Well, open it goddamit."

"We have no key."

"Leave it here and go back to work."

Then Gonzalez who had been gripping the hoe asked, "Why did my wife laugh."

Juan Gonzalez was a gentle, fair-skinned man with a beardless face and features of a handsome Indian. He resembled an Aztec common in those calendars sold in cafes.

Mago smiled and tightened his fists. He turned around and shouted at Gonzalez. The other peasant uttered something beneath his breath. The bastard, Gonzalez thought, he has my wife.

"Leave the box! Now leave!" he shouted, pointing his finger. The men left dragging their feet and soon they became a speck in the horizon. Mago stared at the large black chest. It had a big lock with a big, thick chain around it.

"Elenaaa!!!" he shouted.

The women came running from the house.

24 • Julian S. Garcia

"I said Elena! You go back inside the house."

"What do you want?" she snarled.

"Take this box inside."

"It's dirty, leave it out here."

"Clean it. Now do as you're told, bitch!" She wiped the trunk with her skirt and saw carved etchings of a skull.

"Ave María Purísima!" she cried.

The woman dropped the skirt and ran down the road. Mago was left alone. He shook his head and cursed her.

"You damned bitch!" he shouted. He bent down and picked up the trunk. He saw that it was ancient and had a skeletal design on the lid. He cursed as he dragged the box into the house.

Once inside, Mago heaved the heavy trunk on the kitchen table. Maria, the other woman, had fallen asleep. Elena had gone to the fields with her husband. He was still in the fields near the quarters that housed the peasants.

When Gonzalez saw his woman running down the path, he dropped his sickle and ran towards her.

"*Amor*, the box you found is cursed," she said breathing anxiously as she stared at him under the waning moon.

"It is a gift for Mago. It is good for both of us," Gonzalez said smiling. Elena did not understand his meaning.

"Forget the carvings. It is done for keepsake."

Gonzalez saw her features change as though a sudden thought had twisted the sinews of her heart. She cracked a crooked smile. She did not wait for more talk and left him wordless. Gonzalez stuttered, his syllables falling on the soil.

When Elena climbed through a window into Mago's house, she saw her sister asleep. The room was dirty. Pictures of saints adorned the walls. A thin, silky canopy covered the bed. Elena heard the snoring of a fat whale. She had called Mago a whale behind his back. She hated him and his desires, his rough ways and his animalism. But it was Maria whom Mago loved the most, and it was to her that he would end up giving his treasures. And Gonzalez could give her nothing. He was nothing but a peasant.

Elena tiptoed and passed Mago's room and then saw the trunk on the kitchen table. There was a butcher knife in the sink. The bastard couldn't open the trunk, Elena thought. She picked up the soil-strained knife and suddenly felt a strange vibration strike her bones. All this time, she had thought about stabbing Mago and taking his riches.

But her instincts swayed into another direction. She could not fight her desire to enter Mago's bedroom. She sneaked into the room and saw her victim asleep. He was covered completely, and all she could see was his human form. She hated Mago. She spat at the victim and thrusted the knife into his neck. Again and again, she plunged the tempered steel into the victim.

"You bitch!" Mago cried, "you're killing her."

They struggled and fell onto the floor. Mago was still bewildered and horrified. Elena jabbed the blade into his ribs and Mago cried out, "*Cabrona!*" The blade penetrated his neck and he slumped to the floor. Blood oozed out like thick molasses.

"The gold is mine!!" she hissed.

Mesmerized, she fell and stumbled onto her deed. She had stabbed her sister. Mago laid on the crimson pool, his face buried in a puddle of blood. Maria was soaked on the bed sheets.

"The box!" Elena cried.

When she pried the trunk open, Elena screamed. The peasants returned and found Elena hysterical. Gonzalez had come with the sheriff and then it was discovered that Elena had gone mad. She killed Mago and her sister.

The sheriff looked at the box and told Gonzalez to place the contents in the wagon. Outside, the peasants asked Gonzalez what was inside the box.

"*Memorias!*" Gonzalez said, solemnly.

And when the men saw inside the trunk, they discovered bags of sand. Empty dust, worthless.

Gonzalez turned around and told the peasants, "See what happens when the human spirit becomes greedy. All gold turns to dust because of greed."

ELBA NAZARIO

Enid Sepúlveda

No one saw the black mist coming over the mountain. It had been a long time since anyone in Guayanilla had looked up at the sky. Yayo, the eldest citizen, didn't see it and he had always seen everything. The black mist spread over the tops of the sun baked mountains and poured slowly towards the town. Yayo saw nothing, he closed his eyes and made the sign of the cross over his heart. Then he walked quickly past the cemetery. Today, the family would bury Elba Nazario. He thought of her and shuddered, made the sign of the cross again and hurried home. Her family, watched the coffin go down, down into the opening.

Elba Nazario was being buried today, next to *papá*, the only man who had ever loved her. Close by was her best friend, who had killed herself years before when she found herself pregnant and unmarried. In this place of rest, so close to *La Central*, the now abandoned sugar refinery, so close to the waters of *Ventana*, Elba Nazario would be buried. Her family watched the coffin go down, down into the opening.

She was going into the ground and she was afraid. She knew *papá* was there and her friend too, but still she was afraid. She held on tighter to the still white handkerchief. She had much rather sit on her rocker than be buried. She'd much rather rock all day on that beautiful rocker *papá* had made for her. Since the morning after the night of her wedding, she had rocked in silence. With only the sound of the motion, back and forth, and much later the quiet sounds of the rotting wood, Elba sat day after day and stared at the towns people who still dared walk by. They'd stare at the ground as if they had lost something. Soon no one in town looked up and today only she could see the mist coming. It covered her coffin with a fine film. Lower and lower, she went into the grave. The darkness frightened her but *papá* was there, and soon her best friend would come to talk and comfort her. The dirt was all around her like a tightly fitting dress, she gripped the still white handkerchief in her hand and called to *papá*. She thought of Guayanilla, of Eduardo and of the night of her wedding.

She had never left Guayanilla, she hadn't wanted to ever. Barrio Tamarindo was her home and she loved it. She recalled how warm the waters of the river *Ventana* were in summer and how often she had bathed in the place just near her house. Sometimes in autumn, she'd catch the returning crab and bring some home to mama, who made the best *sopón* in the village. She'd never leave Guayanilla, not for a long time. One night years ago, she went to nearby Yauco to a dance. She met Eduardo Broco. She married him three months later. Other than the night of the dance, she had never left Guayanilla, she never would.

The day she told *mamá* she'd marry Eduardo, *mamá* started to hand make the lace for her white gown. She made the veil and even the handkerchief. *Mamá* didn't care for the ritual of the handkerchief. She often told Elba how awful she had felt on the night of her own wedding and how she had wished she had moved away from the town years ago before Elba became a woman. Elba Nazario reassured her *mamá* that Eduardo loved her and that the ritual must be followed.

The whole town would attend the wedding. It was the day they had all awaited. The women had been starching and ironing the fine linen for the church altar and the tables where the food would be eaten. There was something for everyone to do. Someone was in charge of

28 • Enid Sepúlveda

roasting the young pig. Another had baked the most beautiful wedding cake, another baked the bread and another brought the rum.

The eldest *Abuela* led the children away from the preparations so as to distract them. She taught them games she had played when she was a child, including the wedding game. One boy was the one chosen to tear the muslin cloth into handkerchief size squares, one for each of the girls. The boys watched as the girls flirted and moved their bodies just as *Abuela* had shown them. One girl who was ten, and had played the game before went first . . .

> *arroz con leche se quiere casar*
> *con una nenita de la capital*
> *que sepa tejer, que sepa bordar,*
> *que ponga las cosas en su propio lugar*
> *contigo si, contigo no,*
> *contigo mi vida, me casare yo . . .*

Elba Nazario remembered how carefully she had run her fingers down every pleat in the curtains that covered her bedroom window. She fluffed the pillows on her nuptial bed in her new home. Eduardo had chosen the solid colors of the walls. If she had had a choice, she would have chosen flowers, tiny flowers in all bright colors.

Eduardo had picked the location of the house. The land was perfect for seeding. She thought she'd plant *qandules*, bananas and *acerolas*. In a week or so the ripe mangoes would fall from the tree that was outside the bedroom window. And they were *mayaguezanos*, her favorite type of mango.

She thought again of the reception that night. She knew there would not be enough room for all the town peoples out on the lawn. Some would have to dance and wait outside the gate in the sugar cane field. She had prayed that the moon would not come out, so the guests would leave early. She gripped the perfectly white handkerchief in her hand.

The *Padre*, she recalled, had said it was the best wedding service he had ever delivered and she was the most beautiful bride he had ever seen. He would not attend the reception afterwards because he despised the ritual. Elba did not blame him. Long before, when he first finished seminary school and was assigned to the church in Guayanilla, he had spoken out against the ritual. He told Elba of the night he had walked past the town bar, on the night Brunilda and Pedro were married. He had looked in and had seen Pedro waving the bloody handkerchief for all to see. And how the men had laughed and drank. That night he ran back to the rectory and had wretched, emptying his belly of the *pasteles* and wedding cake. Thereafter the men promised to carry out the ritual outside of town, away from the women and children. Padre Napoleón kissed Elba's face and told her to pray to the Virgin Mary for an early day break, when it would be all over.

Her youngest cousin had stolen the lucky pig's tail, while the pig cooker was not looking and had run to the river. And she remembered also that she had thrown the bridal garter to her eldest cousin, who was over thirty, and had no chance of ever marrying. And mamá had whispered a few reminders in her car, kissed her face and had cried. Elba, Eduardo and the guests left the reception hall after having danced the last *són*, walked past the river, and over the bridge to her new home. Once there, some of the guests positioned themselves outside the door of the house, while others continued to dance on the lawn. Music could still be heard coming from the town. Eduardo waved to the guests, held Elba's hand and they stepped inside.

She had tried so hard to bleed that night as every good bride should have, and to not let Eduardo know that she enjoyed everything he did to her. She tried so much to make this night perfect, but she did not bleed. Eduardo said nothing as he walked out the door, passed the gate and disappeared into the night.

She had said nothing to him but cried into the night and the night went on and on. She tried to forget the look of disappointment on Eduardo's face when he had turned on the lights and saw that the handkerchief was still white.

The guests left quickly, when they saw Eduardo run from the house. Only one drunk and feeble minded old man remained and swore into the night that he had seen the wave of the red. He swore by the Blessed Mother that he had seen the red. And even the people of the higher mountains swore the next morning that they had heard both Elba and the old man cry. No one remembered to say that that night, the wedding night, the island coqui had not sung.

And the next morning Elba cried no more. She walked home. *Mamá* knew everything that had happened and did not say a word when Elba walked on to the porch and sat in her favorite rocker—the one *papá* had made for her. Elba would not take her wedding gown off for days, not until *mamá* threatened to leave her alone in Guayanilla. But she never let go of the still white handkerchief.

Mamá cried with no relief that hot afternoon when Elba decided to die. Many years after the night of her wedding, she decided to die. The town embalmer, had tried to remove the handkerchief from Elba's hand but couldn't. Everyone concerned agreed it was best to leave it in her hand.

Somewhere else in town that day, an old man sat in his chair and looked at the floor and didn't see the mist come in through the holes in the screen door. His wife, drank coffee in the kitchen, the mist wrapped around the legs of the table and her chair.

And the black mist settled over Guayanilla and the townspeople did not see it. It had been so long since any of them had looked up at the sky. The island coqui sang that song it had sung forever in the trees covered with a certain black mist.

ABAJO

Alurista

Abajo, bajotra, jotraba, trabajo, rabajo, ajo

"es todo, total, sin vueltas ni rodeos. de poético no tiene nada ¿ideológico? . . . ¡mucho menos! es lo mas concreto de la vida, después de adan. digo yo, porque hasta el nehanderthal picaba piedra." decía el beto mientras meño se abrazaba la panza de risa." ¡nó pos sí! pero, compadre que metáforas se flechea usté con ese arco de lengua que hace arcabús. le sobran los rollos pa escopetear lunas." el meño andaba buscando chamba ya por mas de tres meses. lo habían despedido pues los contratos de la compañía no salieron como la unión esperaba—"si, pos no, compadre"—continuaba el beto—"esta es la edad de los cavern-ícolas nucleares que se creen mr spock piloteando el 'enterprise' como monos ejecutivos."

una luz inaudita llenó el chevrolet que manejaban. el parque y los árboles cundieron de un rojo majenta que recordaba los amaneceres repletos de hileras de lechuga o carros.

los dos, beto y meño simultaneamente se remontaban a su juventud, a su adolecencia llena de esperanzas y planes para salir del círculo vicioso del trabajo en los campos del agrimonopolio o en las fábricas transnacionales. habían terminado su secundaria y todo lo que veían en frente de sí, decía: ¡adelante!

el meño estaba enamorado y el beto andaba en las mismas. caminando platicaban de sus sendos amores; llenos de vida, llenos de esperanza.

sus botellas, carro y huesos fueron incinerados. el calor incandeciente de la explosión no pudo separar a estos dos compadres que se retiraban al solacio de sus mas gratos recuerdos.

un colibrí moría de la radiación al amanecer de 100 millas.

BETTY

Roberto G. Fernandez

Se encuentra pelando papas y cortando los rábanos con suma delicadeza para con ellos adornar la fuente que servirá de lecho al pavo de Acción de Gracias. Se ha cortado los dedos seis veces. Aunque cree que las cortaduras han sido accidentales, en realidad no lo han sido. En lo más profundo de su ser, Betty desea hacerse daño para así evitar la elaboración de la cena. Se fija y observa que sus heridas son meros arañazos. Sin saber por qué, se siente decepcionada. Se seca las manos con rapidez y se dispone a encender el ventilador que cuelga del techo. Tiene calor a pesar de que no lleva sostenes.

Un ligero viento mece las copas de los árboles y una lluvia de nueces se precipita al suelo. Betty piensa que pronto tendrá que dedicarse a la recolección de nueces para luego prepararle decenas de "pies de nueces" a su esposo. Es una de las pocas cosas que el médico le permite comer.

Betty regresa al fregadero y en voz alta afirma: "Todos los años la misma gente, la misma mierda." Esta noche participarán cuarenta comensales, todos más o menos emparentados. Betty pensó cancelar la cena de este año, mas accedió a las súplicas de su esposo. Este la amenazó con un paro cardíaco. El teléfono suena:

—¿Diga?

—Es Joe Sr., llamo para saber cuántas botellas de vino debemos llevar.

"La misma pregunta de siempre," piensa Betty. ¿Por qué me tiene que hacer la misma pregunta año tras año? Le dan desos de decirle una barbaridad como caca o pipi, pero se refrena.

—Igual número que el año pasado, diez botellas ya que cada botella produce cuatro copas y la mayoría de los invitados consumen dos y los niños beben gaseosa.

—Gracias. Eres un primor. Pero hay que tener cuidado con los refrescos. Asegúrate que el sello metálico no esté quebrado. Recuerda que veinte niños murieron por esta misma fecha el año pasado al beber gaseosas envenenadas con cianuro.

—¡OK!

Joe Sr. tritura con la vista un pedazo de sandía que yace en el refrigerador que ha dejado semiabierto mientras hablaba con su cuñada. Las sandías siempre lo han exitado. Se incorpora, toma el paraguas y se dirige al mercado a comprar el vino más barato que pueda encontrar. Cuando llega, flirtea con la cajera, diciéndole lo hermoso que tiene los pechos mientras le deja caer un billete de cinco dólares por el hermoso canal que forman sus abultadas ubres. Joe Sr. compra diez botellas de un vino californiano a noventa y nueve centavos la botella. Están rebajadas.

Regresa a casa y comienza su anual tarea. Se prepara a quitarle la etiqueta a cada botella para luego pegar las etiquetas de las marcas famosas que ha venido coleccionando durante el año de amigos y conocidos. Durante la cena, de seguro, alabará el aroma y la textura de la selección de este año.

Betty vuelve a la cocina y trata de poner el pavo en el horno. El espacio no es suficientemente grande para aquel cóndor. Betty comienza a pegarle al ave indefensa, a la vez que maldice a su marido por crearle este compromiso de mierda.

Ochenta millas al norte, Joe Sr. continúa encolando las etiquetas, mientras que Nellie, su esposa, se está quejando. Nellie acaba de descubrir que la peluca no le hace juego con el vestido de noche que llevará al convite. Comienza a gritar y a comerse las uñas postizas. Afirma que no irá a la cena. Su esposo no se inmuta. El sicólogo de Nellie le ordenó que no se conmoviera ante los gritos de su esposa, que estaba superando la etapa anal. Chuck, el hijo menor del matrimonio, la tranquiliza. Le dice que es mucho más atractiva y que aparenta menos edad que su cuñada Betty. Nellie tiene sesenta y cinco años e irá a la comida sólo para asegurarse de que lo que dice su hijo es verdad. A pesar de sus inseguridades, Nellie es una mujer piadosa. Acude al culto religioso tres veces por semana, donde generalmente ora por la conversión de Rusia. Hoy rezó por los abisinios. Nellie cree que Dios debe brindarles su ayuda a pesar de que son negros. Nellie tiene un hijo adoptivo en Tailandia por el cual paga veinte y cinco dólares mensuales. A cambio de esta cantidad, Nellie recibe una foto anual y una carta mensual.

El teléfono suena. Es Jimmy. Le dice a su madre que llegará tarde, que tiene un asunto importante que resolver. Betty le suplica que no la haga sufrir más, que se aleje de las malas compañías, que si continúa le va a causar la muerte a su padre. Jimmy cuelga el auricular. Betty, desconsolada, se dirige hacia el baño cuando el teléfono suena una vez más.

—¿Diga?

—Es Frank. No vendré esta noche.

Betty sabe exactamente por qué. Es lo mismo que dice todos los años desde su divorcio.

—Trata de animarte. Pasa después. Te hará bien.

—Quizás pase, pero la felicidad me abandonó el día que me dejó.

Sin duda, Frank vendrá borracho. Es un alcohólico. Frank es hermano de Joe Sr. Su ex-esposa es una cantante frustrada. Se casó con él cuando había dinero, ya no hay más. Lo perdió todo. Tienen cuatro hijos. A instancias de su ex-esposa, la Santa Sede les anuló el matrimonio después de treinta años. Ella cuelga el certificado de anulación de la pared de la sala, y lo alumbra con luz ultravioleta. Ahora tiene un enamorado, pero ella no cree en relaciones premaritales. Por esta razón, perdió a su otro novio. La cantante no participará del pavo de

Acción de Gracias, aunque será tópico de discusión durante la sobremesa.

Está anocheciendo y Betty continúa luchando con el pavo. Está sollozando. No llora por el pavo sino por Blackie que murió hace un año. Se seca las lágrimas y se dispone a ducharse antes de que comiencen a llegar los invitados. Blackie sí la comprendía.

Los festejos están al comenzar. El pavo incómodo trata de observar desde la ventanilla del horno pero se da cuenta que no tiene cabeza. Nellie, aún en el auto, está preocupada. Cree que va a llover. Nellie tratará de convencerlos que la cena se celebre adentro. Nadie le hará caso. Joe Sr. viene ensayando la oratoria anual sobre los valores morales y la libre empresa. Esta noche halagará a los concurrentes con el poema "The Bells" de Edgar Allen Poe, su poeta predilecto.

Joe Jr., su esposa, Mary Kay, y las dos niñas llegan temprano. Ellos no se quedarán a comer. Asistirán a los festejos en casa de los padres de Mary Kay, ricos comerciantes en caramelos que lograron el sueño americano vendiendo confituras italianas. Betty los saluda y piensa si Joe Jr. reventará este año o el próximo. Joe Jr. es una barriga ambulante o una panza con patas. Se acomodan y hablan de la situación en Abisinia, de la inflación y de las condiciones climatológicas. El televisor está encendido durante la conversación. De repente, Mary Kay lanza una mirada a Joe Jr. y éste como si fuera un resorte se incorpora balbuceando: "Es hora de irnos". Al salir él eructa y ella se tira un pedo. Las niñas son muy educadas; ni eructan ni se tiran pedos. Si lo hicieran pedirían disculpas.

Betty se alegra que se hayan marchado. Está algo intranquila. Tiene que limpiar el baño y sus hijos aún no han llegado. Los dos varones viven fuera, la hembra vive en casa. Todos son trentones. Betty piensa si es que tendrá que continuar esta ceremonia tribal el día que su marido se muera.

Se sientan a la mesa. Los asientos están señalados con el nombre del ocupante. La tarjeta también posee el día del cumpleaños de otro miembro de la familia para así facilitar la reconexión familiar. Hay un asiento desocupado para Frank. Aunque no comerá se le sirve "in absentia." A la derecha de la mesa principal hay una mesita para los niños. Estos se están mordiendo y pateando. Los adultos comienzan a pelear en defensa de sus respectivos retoños. Nellie, como una gallina, protege a su nieta proporcionándoles fuertes galletazos a los otros niños. Esto causa un mayor desorden. Quizás Nellie piense que debe proteger a su nieta, quien partirá en el avión de medianoche rumbo a Iowa a casa de su madre.

Ahora todos se encuentran hablando sobre la ex-esposa de Frank. Están de acuerdo que fue un tonto al firmarle la pensión alimenticia. Nellie se vanagloria que su hijo Chuck no la firmó, que no le sacaron ni un centavo, que es un hombre de mucha firmeza. Las miradas se tornan hacia Lil, la hija de Betty, quien ha llegado con su novio árabe. Todos piensan si será negro.

Lil cambia de puesto con su prima Marcia. Quiere sentarse al lado de su primo Chuck.

—Chuckie, un besito para tu prima favorita. Cuéntame cómo te va por allá.

—Bastante bien. Trabajando mucho.

—¿Y esa malparida?

—¿Qué malparida?

—Tu ex. Sabes que no la soporté desde un principio.

—Me imagino le vaya bien. En realidad no me importa.

—¡Y cómo te hizo sufrir! ¿Te hizo sufrir mucho, verdad? Este regalo es para la niña. Pero no quiero que termine en casa de esa mala hierba. Es una muñeca carísma, y hasta quizás la trate de revender y quedarse con el dinero, pero te garantizo que va a morir sola porque eso que te hizo no se le hace a nadie.

—Perdóname Lil pero me están llamando.

—¡Cómo no! Pero regresa en seguida que tenemos mucho de qué hablar.

Chuck se dirige hacia la arboleda de nueces y parece admirar los frutos. Lil se vuelve a acomodar y devora un ala de pavo cubierta con salsa de arándanos. Lil es maestra y le gusta llevar vestidos descotados. Tiene treinta y tres años. Su novio tiene veinte y ocho. Lil jura que su novio jamás le ha puesto un dedo encima. Nadie le cree pero todos defienden su honor. Lil tiene dos hermanos. Uno de ellos es drogadicto y al otro le encantan los penes.

El padre de Lil tiene problemas al masticar. Esta mañana perdió su dentadura postiza. La echó por el inodoro, sin querer. Betty se enfureció tanto que le golpeó. Ella está cansada de cuidar a su marido, piensa que un día los abandonará a todos y se marchará a California. Pero ahora está de anfitriona en la cena. Betty está algo preocupada, pues sus hijos aún no han llegado. Joe Sr. se encuentra recitando "The Bells." Hasta Frankie y Deborah han llegado a tiempo. Deborah no quiere a Frankie, pero no cree que pueda encontrar a otro hombre. Frankie acaba de preparar una ensalada "art deco". Todos se la celebran mucho. Su esposa no dice nada.

Betty escucha el auto de Jimmy y se precipita hacia la puerta. Le suplica que entre por un costado para que nadie lo vea en esas condiciones. Jimmy no le hace caso y de un empellón la tira hacia un lado y prosigue hacia el baño donde huele un poco de cocaína. Luego de salir del baño, se sienta a la mesa desde donde comienza a gritar que no lo hará más. Su nuevo vicio ha reemplazado sus viejos días de masturbador. Jimmy podía masturbarse hasta 10 veces al día. Una vez Jimmy, le contó a su padre la fuerza de su virilidad y éste enorgullecido le refirió el hecho a todos sus amigos.

En este momento, Joe Sr. reza un Padre Nuestro. Luego de terminar la oración da gracias al Señor por haber protegido a la familia durante estos días tenebrosos de iniquidades por los cuales atraviesa la tierra, y añade: "A pesar de habernos visto en el umbral de la necesidad de trabajar en el lodo, nunca nos hemos embarrado. Alabado sea el Señor." Todos responden: "Amén".

La primera gota de lluvia cae sobre la peluca de Nellie y va deslizándose lentamente sobre la sien. Al sentirla, Nellie comienza a dar alaridos. Sabe que el maquillaje comenzará a corrérsele. Aparece Bruce, el hijo mayor de Betty, con un amigo. Todos, a excepción de sus padres, saben que no es un amigo amigo. Sus parientes justifican la conducta de Bruce mediante un hecho que ocurrió hace muchos años. Aconteció que cuando Bruce estaba en cuarto grado, el maestro de geografía le pidió le rascara un grano que le estaba creciendo en la entrepierna. Bruce se equivocó y le rascó otra cosa. Su amigo se llama Dick y vive en Indiana.

—¿Qué es?—dice Dick.

—Pruébalo. Te va a gustar.—responde Bruce.

La cena está tocando a su fin y Frank llega tambaleándose y chocando con cada objeto que se interpone en su zigzag. Frank va balbuceando algo sobre sus antiguos millones. Divisa a su nieta que corretea por el jardín, la agarra de la mano y la obliga a marcar el número de teléfono de su abuela, su ex-mujer. Quiere al menos escuchar su voz. Nadie responde. Frank se acerca a la cabecera de la mesa y le dice a Joe Sr. lo mucho que su nieta quiere a su abuela. A duras penas se incorpora y grita lo triste que se siente. Frankie y Deborah tratan de ignorarlo. Deborah se levanta y le suplica que no los abochorne, mientras Bruce, con mucha sutileza, le comunica a Dick que le pellizque la pierna cuando esté listo para marcharse. Dick practica varias veces y en una de ellas va más allá de la pierna y Bruce automáticamente recuerda a su maestro de geografía. Frankie sabe que de seguro tendrá que llevar a su padre a casa, desvestirlo y meterlo en la ducha. Joe Sr. se halla aún recitando "The Bells" y no logra desterrar de su mente la última estrofa del poema. Frank comienza a gritar que a su sobrino le gusta tocar la flauta. Bruce lo mira como si fuera una alimaña.

Está lloviendo a cántaros. Nellie se ha encerrado en el baño y se niega a salir. Ha perdido todo su maquillaje, dándole aspecto de momia desteñida. Frank le suplica que le abra la puerta, que está a punto de vomitarse. Deborah le pide que abra y le ofrece un velo para cubrirse. Cuando Nellie accede al fin es demasiado tarde. Chuck se encuentra llorando bajo el árbol de pacana. Lil, ansiosa, espera que esta noche se consuma su amor. Betty desesperada por la ausencia de Blackie se ha herido con el cuchillo mientras le cortaba un trozo de pavo a su marido. Fue un accidente. Bruce, al ver el charco de sangre, llama a la ambulancia. La herida es lo suficientemente profunda para recibir siete puntadas. Joe Sr. ha caído al piso obsesionado por el poema, mientras que el otro lado del pueblo Joe Jr. y Mary Kay eructan y se tiran pedos. El árabe hace ademanes de levantarse y Lil le suplica que se quede. En el forcejeo, se le han metido a Lil las bragas dentro del sexo. Cae al piso quejándose, gimiendo y tornando los ojos en blanco. Todos piensan que sufre de un ataque epiléctico. Deborah reconoce que no es un ataque. Lo que está sintiendo Lil no lo ha sentido ella hace varios años.

La noche va oscureciendo el crepúsculo y sobre una mesa congestionada se hallan los restos de un pavo decapitado que cree haber escuchado todo:

Tuve que cortarlo a la mitad no cabía qué vestido tan lindo no qué va no nos vamos a casar todavía no puede masticar perdió la dentadura si bajan los intereses quizás el año próximo hear the mellow wedding bells, Blackie, Blackie, Blackie por qué me has abandonado oh the bells, bells, bells what a tale their terror tells. ¿crees que él? ¿crees que ella? la primera vez que quedó en cinta dijo que se había indigestado Dios mío está lloviendo, está lloviendo cálmate mamá ¿y dónde fue que se conocieron? empanízala y donde esté húmedo pués por ahí ja ja ja espero que no esté llorando por ella me dió y no era mi culpa fue de Michael se va a vomitar los más altos al frente no no los más altos atrás y los niños al frenteríanse what a world of merriment their melody foretells Blackie, Blackie oh mi querido Blackie por favor que nadie te vea así in the silence of the night how we shiver with fright estoy casi segura que ya se han acostado a mi me da muchísima pena tú sabes lo del grano y el maestro, ¿no? eso es yuca y esa cabrona se va a casar con un médico no quiere abrir la puerta un velo, un velo ¿será negro? llamen a una ambulancia que se desangra quiere llamar a su abuelita creo que se van a divorciar también yo tenía mucho dinero no te vayas quédate no lo voy a hacer más oh from out of the sounding cells what a gush of euphory voluminously swells que aroma que textura ooohhh ohhhh jijiji hmmmmm hummm aúaúaú uáuáuá ooooooo hz hzzz así así así qué rico ella me lo ofreció y yo no sabía lo que era y ahora lo necesito diariamente it leaping higher, higher with a desperate desire un velo por favor un velo oh Blackie, of the bells, oh Blackie bells, bells, bells córtame un pedazo más grande escríbeme toca bien la flauta, ¿eh?

LOS TISICOS

Mary Helen Ponce

Nina could not remember when she first heard the word *tísico* but thought it was when she was eight, in the late 1940s. One warm May evening she had stood inside el Angel de la Guardia Church in Pacoima to make her confession. Ahead of her, friends of Celia, her older sister, were softly talking yet Nina heard them say:

"*Se va a casar la Celia?*"

"Neh, he's gonna back out"

Porqué?"

"*Está tísca*, . . . she won't be able to have no kids." Nina had stood waiting to hear more but was pushed forward by a rowdy boy who hissed: *muévase.* As she moved into their line of vision the conversation abruptly ended. Inside the dark confessional Nina felt suddenly cold. The skin on her pudgy arms bristled; her ears buzzed. She tried to think of the sins she would soon confess: the venial sins such as snitching on her brother, and the mortal sins, such as eating a hot dog on a Friday, but could not concentrate. She kept thinking of Celia, . . . and the word *tísica*.

Nina thought often of her sister Celia. Sweet, thin Celia who had a cough that would not go away. Celia planned to marry her novio, Ted, in summer. He had recently come to ask for Celia's hand in marriage accompanied by his only relative, Doña Rosario. The adults had sat in the *sala* to discuss the forthcoming wedding when Celia had begun to cough, and cough. Doña Rosario had quickly taken a handkerchief and held it to her mouth. The black eyes, like halfmoons fastened on Celia who continued to cough, the thin shoulders moving up and down in time with her fluttering eyelashes. The aunt declined *el café* and in a curt tone suggested to their *apá* that Celia should first clear her lungs, then think of marriage. When they left they took with them Celia's smile and their mother's good will. The sala remained quiet, the silence broken by Celia's cough. Soon after Ted stopped calling on Celia. The words "June wedding" were no longer said. Nina knew why Ted would not marry Celia. Celia was *una tísica*, tubercular, and unsuitable for marriage. She began to lie awake nights, unable to sleep, counting not sheep but the times Celia coughed each night.

That summer Nina remained indoors on hot days or sat under the grape arbor. She had heard that the sun was bad for *tísicos*. It made the germs spread. She felt safe beneath the arbor made by her father, where the branches shielded her from *el solazo*. She studied the grape clusters and how they hung together: close, tight, so that it was impossible to separate one grape without touching the others. She thought of the clusters as a family. Each grape was distinct yet all were covered with the white film left by the morning dew. She wondered if tuberculosis was like the dew, which touched all the members of a family to make them tubercular. She sat, staring at the green leaves, and at the blue sky overhead, wondering when she would begin to cough.

When in kindergarten she had been called to the nurse's office where a stethescope was held to her chest. Then the nurse asked her to cough.

"Cough?"

"Yes, cough. I want to hear your lungs."

"No, I don't have a cough."

The nurse did not insist. Nina's pounding heart and terrified eyes spoke volumes. She was sent back to Room K with a note to the teacher that said: Nina Garcia should avoid the sun, and skip recess, as the Garcia family was tubercular.

The next week, during recess she was forced to sit on the long wooden bench with others said to be *tísicos* while around them ruddy-cheeked kids played on the monkeybars and at kickball. Nina sat, kicking out at the dirt with the points of her scruffy brown oxfords, trying not to cry. "It's for your own good," the teacher had said, "It's for your own good." Now and then she called out to Chelo and Virgie, caught up in a kickball contest with the boys, but mostly she sat, her feet moving back and forth across the hard dirt, her eyes on the children at play.

That fall Nina turned nine, and began to sing in the church choir. She went with Elizabet, her older sister. At first she sat and watched the singers practice various *Kyries*, *Glorias* and *Sanctus*. Gradually she found her way to Elizabet who held the blue St. Gregory's Himnal low so she could read the music. She memorized the Mass of the angels, *Panis Angelicus, Asperges Me*, and what was to remain a favorite: the High Requiem Mass. She enjoyed singing in a minor key of sharps and flats, especially during the *Dies Irae*, an eerie hymn that made her skin crawl. Each Thursday evening, promptly at seven she would dash out the door and across the open field to the church. That winter she sang at three masses held for *tísicos* who had died at the sanatorium. And then on day Celia came home from the health clinic in nearby San Fernando to say she was being sent to Olive View sanatorium.

It seemed to Nina that everyone in the neighborhood had at least one relative in Olive View. The younger kids often quarreled over who had the most relatives there.

"My brother is in Olive View"

"So's my seester"

"My whole family, *hásta mi tio esta allí*"

"Híjole"

In the barrio, the kids were all fascinated by *los tísicos* at Olive View. Nina begged to be taken to visit Celia, anxious to compare notes with Chelo who insisted *el sanatorio* was like a hotel, and the patients treated as though on vacation. *Como los ricos!* On the way to the sanatorium Nina sat quietly in the back of the 1933 Dodge her father called *el Dodge*, looking at the green lawns and sparkling white buildings called "bungalows." Upon arriving she was told to remain in the car, but once her parents were out of sight, she got off the car, dashed toward the building then stood on tiptoe to look inside.

Nina saw a large room with white metal beds lined up against one wall. Next to these was a small table, similar to a *viuré*. Shiny green linoleum covered the floor. The square windows, bare of curtains, shone antiseptic-clean. The place did resemble a hotel, thought Nina, stretching to get a better look. It was also said that food was brought in three times a day. Hot, delicious food! Not beans and tortillas but bacon and eggs, corn flakes, cookies, and according to Chelo, three colors of jello!! Red, orange and yellow! It all sounded wonderful thought Nina, but why was it Celia cried everytime they left?

Each Sunday morning immediately after the ten o'clock mass, the parade of cars from the barrio to Foothill Boulevard began. All were on the way to visit *los tísicos*. Some families packed *lonché*, as for a picnic. Sandwiches of *salchicha* and Webers bread, *tacos de carne asada, papas con chorizo* and *frijoles* wrapped in snowy-white limpiadores were packed next to jars of *chiles güeritos*. Some people even took along *un radio*, but Nina's mother did not. Neither did she pack a lunch or remain to visit with other families beneath the shade trees that surrounded the sanatorium. She did however pack *una cajita* with *Palmolive*, a jar of *mentolato*, margaritas from their garden, and lemon drops bought especially for Celia at la Tienda Blanca. It seemed to Nina that their lives revolved around the visits to Celia, who had recently begun to spit up blood.

Most of Nina's friends were familiar with the different stages of tuberculosis. They often discussed them while sitting out a game. Chelo and Virgie insisted it began with a cough followed by the spitting of blood. Meño swore it started with *la fiebre*, as with Justo his brother. The fever, Meño said, was then followed by a cough. All agreed that when blood was evident, it <u>was</u> serious. Worse, once a person was hospitalized they would be given *el pnumo*. When all else failed there was *la operación*.

El *pnumo* was said to be white gas, similar to ice cream, that was injected into the lungs with a huge needle. This collapsed a diseased lung so it could heal; the patient then used the alternate lung. Meño said that was why tísicos were always short of breath and weak. When the *pnumo* failed to heal the lung cavities or *ollítos*, then it was time for the doctors to operate.

When Nina heard that Celia was to receive *pnumo* she got a sharp pain in her chest, right where it was said the big, big needles were

48 • Mary H. Ponce

stuck. She was put to bed with the hot water bottle. She dreaded the weekly reports on Celia's condition; she feared hearing the words: *la operación*. All three persons who had died the year she was nine had been tubercular. All had received *pnumo*. All had had an operation. All had died in Olive View sanatorium.

On Sunday, when her parents went to see Celia, Elizabet was left in charge of the family. Unlike Celia, Elizabet was a cheerful, round girl who during the week worked as a secretary in a lawyer's office. She was the family's translator, and an excellent cook. When in charge she spoiled the younger kids by baking "pigs-in-a-blanket:" weiners baked in a thick, buttery crust. She also made *chocolaté* which they drank from heavy chipped cups. Somehow Elizabet made Sunday bearable.

That winter the public health nurse came to the homes of families known to be tubercular and advised them to give their children cod-liver oil to ward off *el tb*. Elizabet lined them up each day, next to the kitchen table that held the oil and cut-up oranges. Nina hated the taste of *la medecina*, and was grateful for the sweet orange that kept her from gagging on the slimy fish-tasting oil, that sometimes dribbled onto her dress, and smelled all day long. Nina hated the smell that reminded her she was different, but as she grew older began to notice that few kids that drank it, coughed.

When Celia did not respond to *el pnumo*, the doctors decided to operate. Elizabet accompanied her parents to Olive View, where the procedure was explained by a tall, pale doctor said to look *igualito que un tísico*. The doctors wanted to experiment on Celia with a new type of operation, Elizabet was told. If allowed, there would be no charge and, they hinted, the hospital bill might be cancelled entirely. This condition was an important one for people of the *barrio* who did not have insurance or savings, who often signed over property to *el gobierno* in return for medical assistance. Perhaps, Elizabet was told, the family might still retain their home.

Nina remembered well the discussion of *el vil*. One evening while drying the supper dishes she had wandered outside to el porche where her parents were sitting, deep in thought. She overheard Elizabet explaining about the operation, and the hospital bill. Her father began to pace back and forth across the cold cement as Elizabet talked in a low, insistent voice. It was common knowledge that many families had lost their homes to *el condado* when forced to sign over property so their *tísicos* could remain at the sanatorium. However, not everyone was honest. The Arballo's, whose two children had been at Olive View had sworn they did not own their home, as did Don Tiburcio who owned two gas stations! They feared losing *la propiedad, la casa*. Others more clever arranged for the transfer of a house-deed to relatives with the condition that it later be returned. Nina's father, however signed *los papeles*. With a firm, steady hand he signed away their home to ensure Celia would have *la operación*.

Celia's operation took place on a dark, cloudy fall day. Later Nina overheard Elizabet say Celia's chest looked like a quilt, full of small stitches. Every Sunday *el Doge* was cranked up and *el aceite* checked. Elizabet no longer dared to miss a visit; Nina was now left to supervise the younger children. They attended early mass, then rushed home to prepare for the visit. Elizabet would scurry around the kitchen, baking cookies and making *lemonada* while their mother stood quietly looking out the window. When all was ready they would climb into the car which her father then backed out past *los pirúles* and onto the street.

After they left Nina would sit under her favorite pepper tree to embroider *fundas*. She liked doing this because she was allowed to choose a design, transfer it to the pillowcase with a hot iron then stitch in the colors of her choice. But the big needle with the colored thread no longer obeyed her command. She stitched at random, thinking of Celia and the stitches on her skinny chest. At the end of the day she was surprised to see the *fundas* stained with blood from her pricked fingers. She folded them, then put them in Elizabet's sewing basket along with the needles and thread. There they remained, untouched.

That winter Nina caught a cold, then pneumonia. She was moved from her small cot to her parent's lumpy bed where she lay, red as a lobster, from the fever that raged through her body, a fever intensified by the fumes of *el mentolato*. When she did not get better her mother sent Elizabet to buy four large potatoes which she cut into thick slices then placed on Nina's chest. The potatoes were said to "bring out" the fever. When they turned black they were removed then replaced with fresh *papas*. They felt cool against Nina's hot chest which in her delirium appeared to have stitches.

Nina recovered in time to be driven to Olive View to say goodbye to Celia. The *operación* had not cured her. Nina was not allowed inside the infirmary so sat in the car parked next to the white bungalow where the year before Celia had been. The building now looked old, the paint was chipped; the windows grey. The lawn and trees were no longer

50 • Mary H. Ponce

green. To Nina, huddled inside the dusty car, the sanatorium no longer resembled a hotel. It now looked desolate, dead.

They buried Celia at Valhalla cemetery, next to Rito and Rosalia, the brother and sister that had died years before. During the Requiem Mass, the *Dies Irae* sounded dull, and flat to Nina who stood next to Elizabet, the younger children next to her. Now and then Nina thought she was about to cough, but did not. Elizabet, who understood everything, held her hand tight as tears rolled down her pale cheeks.

Somos tísicos, Nina thought with a sigh. Diseased . . . like the grapes. The film of tuberculosis has touched us all. I'll probably be next, or Elizabet. Or maybe, just maybe the cod-liver oil would deliver them from *el pnumo, la operación*. She looked at the younger children, at their ruddy cheeks, bright eyes and tough young bodies.

Perhaps we're not like the grapes after all Nina thought, but like the grape leaves in the arbor. Some drop off while others grow and spread out. She consoled herself with this thought while in the front pew her mother and father huddled together.

When the priest raised his hand for the final blessing Nina looked toward the coffin, toward Celia, sweet Celia who was now only a memory.

Celia who had lived and died, . . .*tísica*.

Dedicated to the memory of my sister Rosalia (whom I never knew) and my brother Rito (whom I barely remember).

DIMANCHE

Gloria Velasquez Treviño

fragmento de *Soldaditos y muñecas*

Hay momentos precisos en la vida que no se borran, se guardan en un rincón olvidado del corazón, allí lejos de la realidad y en aquellos momentos de triste lluvia cuando ni el presente ni el futuro parecen existir, se sacan uno tras uno y se goza lentamente de su sabor dulce y amargo. Me recuerdas de vez en cuando. ¿Raúl? Recuerdas aquellas noches tiernas en el van del Cowboy cuando me besabas con una pasión insorportable, los dos perdidos en otras realidades. Me tocabas suavemente el pelo, los senos llenándome con esperanzas y promesas hasta que las maldiciones de Mercitas que luchaba contra las manos agarronas del Cowboy interrumpían nuestro éxtasis. Entonces volteabas y sonriendo les decías. "Be cool. Be cool." Pasábamos toda la noche estacionados allí a un lado del camino de tierra escuchando la música de los Beatles y los Stones hasta que nos cansábamos y nos salíamos para afuera a interrumpir el silencio mágico del campo. Subíamos la radio y te ponías a bailar el stroll con el Cowboy y sus perros mientras que Mercitas y yo nos fumábamos un cigarro, dejando soltar de vez en cuando unas risas profundas que desaparecían sobre los montes. Años después en aquel apartamento sombrío, buscaríamos con desesperación aquellas risas, congeladas ya por el tiempo. Y ahora, Raúl, tan lejos de mí, en los brazos de otra, ¿piensas en todo eso? Suspiras mi nombre con nostalgia o me maldices al recordar aquella desolada mañana cuando enterramos al difuntito que por tanto tiempo habíamos esperado. No te podía ver el rostro por las gotas frías que nos empapaban de dolar y los gritos de la gente que nos recordaban aquella noche cuando me habías golpeado y dejado como muñequita rota en el piso, la sangre escurriendo, gritándome puta por haberte encontrado en los brazos de otra. Después en el hospital delante de los médicos me habías suplicado que to perdonara, "Esperanza, estaba borracho, no sabía lo que hacía." Habías llorado entonces como no pudiste hacer aquel día parado delante de la lose fría del niño que nunca sentimos. Tanto, tanto te quise Raúl. Tanto, sin poder decírtelo, a pesar de tus esperanzas, a pesar de tu inocente inocencia. Soñador maldito. "Amar, vivir, viajar, ser algo grande en la vida," me decías. Y como tonta, me dejé volar, me dejé llevar por tu alma a lugares mágicos. Momentitos momentáneos. Maldita soñadora soy yo vagando ahora con los pies hinchados y el alma herida por las calles vacías buscándote con una loca pasión en cada rostro que veo. La ciudad me suspira tu nombre. Entro a las Tres Tortugas. Tomo una, dos, tres cervezas. Cojo la pluma. Escribo uno, dos, tres versos tristes, pero ya no apareces. Entro a los museos, a librerías. Escucho los comentarios de los intelectuales retóricos pero no oigo nada, sólo este latido, que triste en mi corazón, sique repitiendo tu nombre. Desolada, camino por la Alameda. Me siento en un banco, pero no escucho las voces mudas que me suplican, "Olvídalo, olvídalo. Ve a Cuauhtemoc, los Niños Héroes, los muertos de Tlatelolco." Subo, me bajo de camiones. Por dondequiera ando en busca de tu imagen hasta que por fin la encuentro flotando muerta, solitaria sobre el Lago de Chapultepec donde no hace tanto me abrazaste y prometimos no olvidarnos nunca. Es entonces cuando, parada allí, rodeada por las sombras y las tristes voces de los muertos, me rondan los versos amargos que escribí aquel triste día de domingo como este:

54 • Gloria V. Treviño

Dimanche

profond,
trou rectangulaire
dans le cimetière,

vide,
bouteille jeté
par un homme désillusionné,

pourpre,
meurtrissures gravées
sur le bras de la mère.

épaisse,
larmes de la femme
dans le mioroir,

Jour éternel,
comme le vent
me ployait
et me poursuit.

Todo es una maldita repeticion. —Tu prima Mercedes murió anoche—. Mentiras, puras mentiras. Maldigo, piso la lluvia sonriente hasta sentirla llorar de dolor. Cruzo calles desconocidas. Túneles oscuros. Evito los rostros desilusionados de los hombres que, con su triste olor a tantas borracheras, se recargan en las esquinas. Dejo que la lluvia me empuje hacia una calle oscura, unos apartamentos sucios. Subo unos escalones oscuros y hediondos. Toco a la puerta. Una señora me contesta, Dizque se ahogó en la contesta noche y como tenían la música muy recio, nadie se dió cuenta. Hallé su número en su cartera. Raúl, allí en el sillón, meado, la cabeza torcida, las babas escurriéndole hasta el piso. —"I can't stop loving you. I've made up my mind to live in memory of a broken heart". ¿te gusta Ray Charles?—. Olvidar esa vieja melodía, las recorridas de noche para sacarlo de bars, de Halfway Houses—Eres la única que me quiere, Esperanza. Corro al pasillo. Vomito sobre unas latas apachurradas, también abandonadas como aquellas almas desamparadas de la esquina. Confundida, me encuentro otra vez en las calles. Los golpes fuertes de la lluvia me hacen pisar fuerte sobre los charcos sucios hasta que me siento apachurrarlos, destruirlos. Respiro profundamente. Saludo al señor de la esquina. Finjo, platico de miles estupideces, sí, posiblemente llueva mañana. No, no supe que ganaron los Boston Celtics. Compro un periódico. Repaso los want ads, my horoscope: SINGLE MAN WANTS SINGLE WOMAN. TODAY YOU WILL BE OPTIMIS-TIC. DEAR ABBY, MY WIFE DOESN'T WANT TO HAVE SEX ANYMORE. Regreso al front page: MEXICAN MAN FOUND DEAD. CAUSE OF DEATH: SUFFOCATION. THIS RAISES THE FIGURE TO 2 MILLION MEXICANS WHO DIED OF ALCOHOLISM LAST YEAR. ACCORDING TO DR. AIDONKER OF STANFORD UNIVERSITY, A REKNOWNED SPECIALIST IN DISEASES THAT AFFLICT HISPANICS, ALCOHOLISM IS HEREDITARY AND CAN BE TRACED TO A DISORDER THAT MEXICANS CONTRACT AT THE STAGE OF PUBERTY.

Me levanto el día siguiente. Ojeo el calendario. Hoy es martes, mañana es miércoles, a las nueve me desayuno, a las diez rezo. Me pongo el impermeable y me digo, "Esta lloviendo fuerte." Salgo con prisa. Camino por todas partes, perdida, confusa como todos los letreros que se me enfrentan, BURGER BOY, CHRISTIAN SCI-ENCE BOOKSTORE, LIVE SEX SHOW, PET GROOMING. "Mundo superficial," me digo, apretándome el impermeable al sentir el frío de las gotas pesadas que me lastiman mi cuerpo delgado. Doblo la misma esquina. Llego a los mismos apartamentos. Subo unos esca-lones susios con aquel fuerte olor. Vomito sobre unas latas vacías. Toco a la puerta. La misma señora tuerta, Mercitas extendida en la cama. Desesperada, busco aquellos mechones largos y lisos, los versos román-ticos de Smokey Robinson. Dizque se ahogó en la noche, se tomó una botella entera de alcohol, andaba borracha. Ya le hablé a la chota. Trato de evitar su mirada, aquel ojo torcido que parece querer escapár-sele. Tranquilizarme, eso es. Sonreírle a la policía, Yes, I was with her last night. No, she wasn't pregnant. Malditas hormigas. Controlarme, caminar despacio, sí señora, hasta mañana señora. Brincar para no pisar las gotas gruesas que se resbalan de mi rostro angustiado. Evitar los ojos negros del día que me siguen de un lado a otro. Saludar al señor de la esquina, sí posiblements llueva toda la semana. Comprar el periódico. Repasar los want ads, Daily Horoscope: SINGLE WOMAN WANTS SINGLE MAN. TODAY YOU WILL BE PESSI-MISTIC. DEAR ABBY, MY HUSBAND DOESN'T WANT TO

56 • Gloria V. Treviño

HAVE SEX ANYMORE. Regresar al front page: MEXICAN WOMAN FOUND DEAD. CAUSE OF DEATH: SUFFOCATION. THIS RAISES THE FIGURE TO 2.1 MILLION MEXICANS WHO DIED OF ALCOHOLISM LAST YEAR. ACCORDING TO DR. AIDONKER OF STANFORD UNIVERSITY, A REKNOWNED SPECIALIST IN DISEASES THAT AFFLICT HISPANICS, ALCOHOLISM IS HEREDITARY AND CAN BE TRACED TO A DISORDER THAT MEXICANS CONTRACT AT THE STAGE OF PUBERTY.

Maldita repetición todo esto. Huyo a las sombras familiares, a los callejones meados donde las ratas gordas me esperan con ansias. Me acomodo en el mismo rincón. Les ruego y ruego hasta que por fin se me acercan. Estiro el brazo. Dejo que se me suban hasta el cuello. Siento sus rasguños y las gotas de sangre que se escapan de mi cuerpo herido. Me acuesto. Esta noche, por primera vez, duermo tranquila.

PAREJA

Juan Bruce-Novoa

para Arnaldo Coen

Se amaban y más que nada querían ser uno — qué horrendo lugar común, eso de *querer ser uno*; pero cualquier lugar común, cuando se le aúna una verdadera pasión, puede traspasar el límite de lo aceptado para conducirnos al extremo de lo increíble, al margen de lo inefable. Y el amor de ellos era una pasión loca — las palabras no ayudan nada, tan gastadas que apenas se arrastran con los siglos encima, como una moneda pasada de mano en mano hasta perder toda imagen que la distinguiera y quedarse inútilmente un recuerdo de otra verdad. Ni modo. La suya era un pasión loca.

En el camino hacia el horror pasaron por los episodios bien conocidos por los lectores de novelas rosas, los aficionados a las cursis telenovelas de SIN, o los que, por su misma cuentan, han sufrido un amor de juventud. Sólo les distinguía la intensidad, no los hechos en sí.

Esto tal vez desvirtúe su amor a los ojos de los algunos — estamos tan acostumbrados a dar más valor a lo anormal — pero tiene la ventaja para mí de que puedo referir a los lectores a fuentes conocidas o contar con su experiencia propia para los detalles y datos de fondo que casi siempre son necesarios en un relato de esta índole y así de esta manera ahorrar mucho tiempo y espacio que me hubiera consumido el pasar por territorios banales. Sólo quisiera subrayar que hacia el final, hablar con ellos era de lo más difícil, porque todo era lo mismo: felicidad, amor, ensimismamiento de los dos en los dos. La única nota negative era la separación.

No quiero decir que se hayan separado por algún tiempo, no. Si les faltó un lugar común fue ese: jamás se separaron por ninguna de las múltiples peripecias que amenazan a los amantes. Fue un romance sin disturbios. Más bien me refiero a la separación esencial: dos personas son, inevitablemente, dos. El amor puede ser uno; ellos pueden ser objetos del verbo *amar*; pueden desaparecer en la inconciencia del arrebato sexual; hasta pueden haberse sumergido en la filosofía erótica de autores perversos como Bataille, Marcuse, Klossowski, o Sade — como en efecto mis amigos habían hecho, leyéndolos juntos y en voz alta, igual que a Emmanuele, Réage, y de Berg — para comprender y asimilar esa necesidad de abandonarse a la pérdida de cualquier conciencia centralizadora y aislante que llamamos el Yo . . . pero siempre regresaban a lo mismo: eran, una frente al otro, dos.

Repetían continuamente:

— Quisiera ser uno contigo.

— Yo también, amor.

Y no se cansaban jamás de ello, porque en la intensidad de la pasión, claro, la repetición es permisible, quizás obligatoria, no sé. Pero ellos ne se daban cuenta. Les desesperaba toda situación que pudiera introducir entre ellos un objeto opaco. La distancia — y hablo de unos pocos metros por lo común, o en casos extremos, tal vez diez o quince máximo — la salvaban con la mirada. Luego descubrieron la estrategia de localizarse frente a un espejo, por si acaso la línea directa les fuera obstaculizada por algún insensible, siempre tendrían la alternativa de encontrarse en el juego de vértices del tercer ángulo de un triángulo visual.

En fin . . . basta de ejemplos, creo que se me entiende. Eran inaguantables, ingenuos, cursis, todo lo que se puede decir de los amantes serios, pero a la vez, inofensibles. Nadie sospechaba que

60 • Juan Bruce-Novoa

pudieran llegar a más. No creo que ni ellos lo hayan intuido, a pesar de todo. Pasó, punto.

Una tarde, en la sala de su departamento, entre besos y caricias, se quedaron desnudos. Repetían lo de siempre: te quiero; yo también; quisiera ser uno contigo; y yo también, amor . . ., mientras se acercaban a ese punto de desaparición de las conciencias enemigas. La coordinación de la intensidad sensual era perfecta gracias a los meses de práctica; llegaban al climax como un solo animal, en eso sí que habían logrado la meta. El sexo era para ellos casi un acto onanista, eran tan uno dentro de la sex/sensualidad transcendente . . . Y se dejaron ir, ansiosos . . . ¿éxtasis, lo sublime, la nada, orgasmo? ¿Cuál palabra no acusa su propia ineficencia en este campo? Todas son la traición misma porque marcan la distancia entre el hecho y la vuelta al mundo consciente de la separación. Estaban en el ser; eran un puro estar. Allí, en ese espacio inefable, inlocalizable, aunque surge de la conjunción de los cuerpos; allí comienza y termina la imposiblidad del cuento, de la narración objetiva. Tal vez tengan razón los místicos al decir que el horror es el grado del amor que nadie aguanta: dios.

(Los sonidos, que siempre parecían ser lo primero que regresaban para orientarlo, le dijeron que el tocadiscos seguía tocando la misma canción. Sin embargo, ella lo sentía todavía duro y dentro, como si él la hubiera tragado para siempre. A su vez, él sabía que se quedaba alrededor de ella, tan firme y penetrante como cuando ella la penetró. Buscó su mano, pero se encontró una que reflejaba la suya en casi todo. Ella abrió los ojos, vio el techo y sintió un temor solitario comenzar dentro de él. La buscó, pero no lo encontraba; él se había desaparecido, dejándolo solo, acostada allí donde momentos antes la había tenido dentro de ella. Miró alrededor, alarmada, sabiendo ahora que él se había quedado sola, único, centrada en ese cuerpo igualmente singular. Se buscó los ojos en el espejo que le devolvió la mirada de ese desconocido muy familiar, ese ser deseado hacía tanto tiempo: la ellos singular y perfecto. Sonrió con los labios sensuales que atraían a tantos hombres; riéndose con la voz profunda que lo distinguía. Se acarició un muslo con la mano derecha, el pecho ambiguo con la izquierda, con verdadero deseo, amor. Lloró — ¿feliz? — su unión, la realización de la meta y del amor; se encontraba sola/o.)

Corrieron voces viles que alegaban que ella lo había matado; otras replicaban que la víctima, más bien era él, porque ella lo había abandonado y que se veía tan solitario. Lo que sí afirmaban todos sin duda era que en ambos se reflebaba la pena de la separación, tan cambiados que se veían. Unos y otros insistían en haber visto a ella o a él por allí, pero jamás podían estar absolutamente seguros de a cuál de los dos. Habían llegado a parecerse tanto, como una pareja después de años de casados, o como un amo y su perro. Mas lo que nunca llegaron a explicarse los románticos—a los cínicos ni les preocupó—fue por qué nunca volvieron a verlos juntos.

DESTINATION

Richard W. Kimball

Three old Penitente crosses stood at the top of a small hill near the tiny New Mexican village called La Pizca. Behind the hill, the high rocky peaks of the Sangre de Cristo mountains loomed menacingly over two freshly dug holes near the base of the rough crosses. The holes, nearly identical, were surrounded by mounds of crusty red soil shoveled neatly about them. One had a finished look, but a pile of dirt still waited at the bottom of the other. The holes were six feet deep, three feet wide and six feet long. Leaning out of the unfinished one was a crude homemade ladder of cedar.

The late afternoon sky over the mountains was rapidly being covered by large and dark clouds that snapped with electrical fire. Though the air already smelled of ozone and rain, the storm had not yet collected over the baking adobe homes of La Pizca.

Two men, their arms burdened with firewood, emerged from a

clump of piñon near the top of the hill and headed down toward the village. Their faces were young and deeply tanned and they walked slowly and purposefully down the old worn trail.

As they neared the place where the crosses stood, one of the young men stopped abruptly. "¿Qué es? Juan Carlos—these holes! Who dug them?"

His companion shrugged. "These?" He laughed weakly. "El tonto viejo has been digging here for more than two weeks. A fool called Filadelfio."

"But why? . . . what for?"

"We can only guess, Tomás," answered Juan Carlos. "The reason . . . ¿quién sabe? The old fool never answers questions."

Tomás studied the holes and said, "They look very much like graves. Who would want to be buried out here?"

"I, too, have wondered," said Juan Carlos. "Filadelfio has no one to bury, except . . . himself."

"Has he told anyone about this digging?"

"No one," Juan Carlos answered, "or very few. One month ago, I remember, he mentioned that he would finish something very important at sunset on this very day. He said he would dig one hole for himself. The other . . . the other for the rest of us."

"Strange," said Tomás. "What else do you know about this old man? What is he like?"

"He is muy misterioso," sighed Juan Carlos. "We often hear him doing carpentry work inside his house. No one knows what it is he makes."

Tomás frowned and said, "You said he was an old man. How old is he? I want to know what he is like."

"No one knows his age—he may be nearly ninety." Juan Carlos pushed some dirt into a hole with the toe of his boot. "He may kill himself yet, though working on these holes up here." He glanced up at the sky. "It's getting cloudy. Let's get moving before it rains. I'll tell you more on the way."

The young men started back down the hill.

"This Filadelfio," Juan Carlos went on, "still calls himself one of the old Penitente Brothers. He says he was once crucified on one of the very crosses we stood beneath. That may be true. He has strange scars, like nail holes, in the palms of his hands and his back is marked as if it had been beaten by thorny cactus whips. It makes him bitter, he says,

64 • Richard W. Kimball

when more and more of the villagers forget the old ways. He is always telling us how sinful we are. But he himself is a very selfish man. He never shares or does a favor for anyone. And he never asks for anything either. He always says, 'Go away! I do not need you!' For years we have ignored him—until he started digging those strange holes."

Tomás said, "I want to stay with you in La Pizca until it gets dark. I want to see the end of this mystery."

No more was said as the men ended their walk. They piled the firewood they carried against the side of Juan Carlos' house before they entered the adobe home. Faint thunder rumbled from the clouds crowding in among the mountain peaks.

Inside another adobe dwelling, near the foot of Penitente Hill, a hammer could be heard rapping against wood. After a while it stopped and an ancient man pushed the creaky door open and came outside to look at the sky. After carefully closing the door, the old man placed a dirt-encrusted spade over his shoulder and very carefully walked up the hill to the crosses.

The man's parchment-like skin was as wrinkled as the bark of the piñon trees he passed. His long white hair hung loose and blew in the wind like flattened pine needles.

As Filadelfio neared the crest where the crosses stood, he stopped and genuflected before them. His narrow black eyes stared straight ahead as he crossed himself in front of the gaping holes. He leaned upon his spade for a few moments to regain his breath and then climbed down the cedar ladder into the unfinished hole.

Stiffly, slowly, old Filadelfio cleared the remaining soil from the excavation with a series of small, painful shovelfuls. After several minutes of such work, he carefully studied the sides and bottom of the hole. It was satisfactory. If he was pleased, he did not show it. His leathery face only tightened into more wrinkles.

Filadelfio climbed out. As he stepped over the edge, he stumbled and knocked the shovel back into the hole, causing clumps of earth and dust to fall in. Snapping about to see the damage, the old man's black eyes flashed with the anger of lightning in the mountains, but he uttered no curses. Instead, he climbed back into the hole to shovel out the debris. He worked slower than before.

Before leaving the hole for the second time, he threw the spade away from the opening. Then he carefully climbed the ladder and got out. He pulled the ladder from the hole and carried it back down the hill to his house in the village. As he went inside his home, a bright flash of lightning streaked across the sky and a crash of thunder muffled the sound of his closing door. Only one small section of open sky remained over the village of La Pizca.

Some of the villagers had noticed Filadelfio coming down the hill. First a few, then many villagers assembled outside his door, talking excitedly in muted tones. Occasionally, they heard strange scraping and shuffling noises within the old man's adobe home. Suddenly the door swung open. The frowning Filadelfio glanced about sharply and propped the door open with a small stick. He went back into his house, ignoring the people outside. The scraping sounds were heard again.

When Filadelfio reappeared, he was pulling a large object through the door. It was a long, wooden box. A coffin! The villagers' faces reacted with horror. All movement within the crowd stopped; all eyes became fixed upon the box.

The coffin was plain and rough. Made of native pine, it was well built and the top was nicely fitted. Sturdy rope handles had been firmly fastened to each side.

Immediately, questions crossed the mind of everyone in the crowd. "Was anyone in the box? . . . Who? . . . If it was empty, who was to fill it?"

The old man loaded the box on an old rugged two-wheeled cart and began to pull it up the hill. Its wooden wheels bumped noisily over the rocks and ruts of the trail. The villagers followed at a polite distance.

Tomás, who hiked beside Juan Carlos, spoke softly. "Perhaps there is only one answer to all of this," he whispered. "He is very old. You say he has always done everything for himself. He must be about to . . ."

"Shhhhh," Juan Carlos interrupted. "Be quiet and wait. We shall know the truth soon."

Reaching one of the two holes, which could now be called graves, Filadelfio gently placed the coffin near the edge. Then he quickly turned around, glared at the milling crowd and immediately started pulling his cart back down the hill. A few villagers followed after him, but most stayed near the graves, staring at the rude coffin by the hole.

Once Filadelfio was out of sight, Juan Carlos and Tomás ventured nearer to the wooden box and tried to open the cover. They slid it open a crack, then all the way and looked in. There was nothing inside. It was just an empty pine box. They closed the lid quickly as a few drops of angry rain slammed into the dusty ground around them.

Some of the villagers began to leave as the rain increased, but a young boy came running up the hill. "He is coming!" he gasped. "He is coming back!" The boy's chest heaved as he blurted, "And he is bringing another coffin! Another just like this one!"

The villagers waited until Filadelfio came into sight, hauling his rickety cart with another wooden box upon it. The old man seemed to be in a trance. His eyes remained fixed upon the ground before him. He walked slowly, oblivious to the heavy rainfall, and pulled his heavy cart with its ominous cargo toward the crowd of anxious villagers. He seemed to move more and more slowly with each step. Halfway up the climb, he stumbled and collapsed on the trail; the coffin slid off the cart into the mud.

"He is dead! Filadelfio esta muerto!" But old Filadelfio was not dead—yet. He struggled to his feet and got up. His pain-racked face reflected his suffering as he strained with the muddy pine box.

Tomás wanted to help the old man, but Juan Carlos held him back. He knew that Filadelfio would want to be left alone.

No longer able to put the coffin back on the cart, Filadelfio began to push it—an inch at a time—up the hill. He had to stop often to rest. The rain began to beat harder as the storm moved in over the valley.

Filadelfio finally pushed the coffin to the side of the second grave. Lightning projected shadows of the old wooden crosses across his handiwork. He gently aligned the second coffin to a place beside the other hole and wiped the top with his ragged sleeve. He had surprised everyone. He had exhibited strength no one thought he possessed.

Filadelfio then stepped over to his first coffin, opened the lid, and climbed in. He held the top open with his old disfigured hands and gazed toward the west.

It was still raining, but thin streaks of light appeared along the southern and western edges of the mountain range. The fast dispersing clouds were beginning to reveal the blood-red sun. Filadelfio watched the sunset for a long time and many villagers did the same. When the sun disappeared behind the edge of the mountains, there was another sound of faraway thunder. It had almost disguised the sound of the coffin lid as it slammed shut. The villagers all knew what had happened. Several crossed themselves nervously.

The noise of thunder became more and more distant as they

turned their attention to the other coffin. No one except Filadelfio knew what it contained. Tomás approached it warily and hooked his fingers under the edge of the lid. He lifted the heavy pine cover gingerly and peered in. Juan Carlos looked in. All of the villagers looked in.

Inside was a long mirror!

FLORENCE AND THE NEW SHOES

Magdalena Gallegos

The sun poked its face through the window and woke Florence out of a wonderful dream. She always dreamed that she could fly and she visited faraway and exotic places. She laid on her back and rubbed her eyes to take the sleepiness away. She traced the cracks on the ceiling, making out strange creatures and animals. The smell of fresh tortillas woke her up completely. She jumped out of her small cot and stood on the bare wooden floor. Out of the black trunk, at the foot of her bed, she picked a red dress with white flowers. She exchanged it for the flour sack nightgown she was wearing. It was August and her bare feet did not feel undressed or neglected for not having shoes.

Florence spun around like a top to see how high her dress would go. She felt happy to be living in this wonderful big house. It was not at all like the one room shack they had left behind. She could remember the cold winter when her mother filled the cracks in the walls with rags. The nights were especially cold. Everyone in the family slept close together with their clothes on in order to keep warm. Florence's mother would tell stories until everyone fell asleep. Florence's favorite was *The Little Match Girl*. It was the story of a little girl who did not have a place to stay so she slept on a street corner. She had one box of matches and at night, she would light a match to try to warm herself. After hearing this sad story, Florence was thankful for having the shack, even if it was cold and ugly.

Florence and her family were farmworkers. They had followed the seasonal work from town to town ever since she could remember. Florence had four brothers: Bennie, Vincent, Tom and Joe. She had one younger sister named Margaret. Her mother's name was Lucy Torres. Joe had told her that their father had died of pneumonia when Florence was a little girl. They were living in Rhode, New Mexico at the time. Soon after that, an uncle, who was a foreman on a farm in Greeley, Colorado, sent the family money to join him. When they arrived, the uncle put them all to work in the beet fields and he gave them a one room shack to live in. Joe told Florence, many times, that he hated his uncle for being so mean. Their uncle lived in a nice big house with nice furniture. Sometimes Joe would get so mad, he would burst out crying. There were times when he got mad at Florence because she did not cry.

By the end of that year, Florence saw her oldest brother Bennie grow up overnight. That is when a farmer hired him as a foreman and moved the whole family to Keensburg, Colorado, where they were now living.

Florence skipped into the kitchen singing, *"Buenos Días, Paloma Blanca*. Morning *Mamá*. Can I help you roll tortillas?"

"Good morning, *Hija*. Try to talk more English so that when you go to school, the teachers will not get mad at you."

Florence thought that English must be pretty important because she had observed her mother and Mrs. Stremel trying to teach each other English. Every day, Florence's mother would take beans, chile and tortillas to Mrs. Stremel's house and Mrs. Stremel would give

Mrs. Torres some of her German food. They communicated with the English words they had heard and pretty soon they were talking to each other in broken English. Mrs. Torres picked up some German and Mrs. Stremel learned some Spanish. Florence thought it might be good to know more than one language.

Mrs. Torres kissed Florence on the forehead. She handed her a small wooden rolling pin and a small wad of dough. Florence knelt on a bench next to her mother, and began to roll and turn the tortilla faster than Florence's eyes could follow. The tortilla grew rounder and thinner with every turn. Florence tried to imitate her mother's motions and in two flips, her tortilla landed on the floor.

"*Dios te bendiga,*" cried her mother, forgetting her English. She picked up the tortilla and threw it away. "You are always in such a hurry. Making tortillas is an art and you must learn it well."

After breakfast was over and the boys had gone to the fields, Florence and her mother washed the dishes and put everything away.

"Florencita, you can go outside and play while I put Margarita to sleep."

"*Bueno, Mamá,*" said Florence and she flew out the door.

Mrs. Torres looked out the window. "*¡Virgen Santisima!* She looks like a wild colt in a red dress," she thought to herself.

Before noon, Mrs. Torres opened the screen door and yelled, "Florencita, *ven aquí,* Come and get me some water."

Florence appeared from behind the barn and ran to get the pail that her mother was holding. The house had no running water, but there was an iron pump out by the barn. Florence had made a game out of getting water. She liked to ride the long pump handle up and down while singing:

"*Abajo al suelo. Arriba al cielo. Agua invisible, aparéceteme.*
(Down to the ground. Up to the sky. Invisible water, appear
to me.)
Abajo al suelo. Arriba al cielo. Agua invisible, aparéceteme."

After a few ups and downs, the water gushed out of the spout and filled the bucket. Florence struggled with the heavy bucket spilling water as she approached the door. The screendoor slammed as Florence carried the water into the kitchen.

"Florencita, one of these days you will break the door down."

Mamá, how did you know it was me? You didn't even turn around."

"*Tengo ojos atras de mi cabeza*," her mother answered.

"If you do, let me see them," Florence said as she strained to catch a glimpse of the hidden eyes beneath her mother's black braided hair.

Mrs. Torres turned around and continued, "Now that you are here, I want to talk to you. The teacher from school came by this morning and said that you are old enough to go to school now. That means that you must have a pair of shoes. All the boys and girls wear shoes to school. Your brothers are going to town today and I will ask them to buy you a pair of shoes."

Florence sat down and put her elbows on the table. She cupped her cheeks in her small brown hands and wondered about this thing called school.

"Do I have to go to school, *Mamá*?" Florence asked her mother. "Do I have to wear shoes?" she continued.

Florence was filled with mixed emotions about school and shoes. It frightened and excited her at the same time. She had seen some beautiful black shiny shoes in a Montgomery Wards catalogue in the outside toilet. She had dreamed of having a pair for her very own. Now, maybe her wish would come true.

Just then, Joe came into the kitchen. He had a piece of string in his hand.

"*Vamos a ver*. Let me measure your feet," He said to Florence.

He measured the string to one of her feet and cut the piece off with his pocket knife. Putting the string in his pocket, he went out the door saying, "*Ahora voy a la tienda con mis hermanos*. We will be back later."

Florence came back from her daydreams and flew out the door.

Later that evening, Florence's brothers returned. The four boys stomped into the kitchen laughing and joking about something that had happened in town. Joe had a brown box under his arm and as he came through the door, he handed it to Florence, saying, "Here are your shoes *manita*."

Florence opened the box with expectations and stared down at the

74 • Magdalena Gallegos

boy's hightop work boots lying in the box. Florence's voice broke as she said to Joe, "There must be some mistake. They must have given you the wrong box."

But no, there was no mistake. Florence heard her brother say, "These are your school shoes."

Florence fought to keep the tears from spilling out of her eyes and her heart felt like it would break.

She looked at her mother pleadingly and said, "*Mamá, dile a Jose que se equivocó*. Tell him he made a mistake. He was supposed to get the pretty black shoes."

Mrs. Torres looked sad and did not know what to do. Then she gave a sigh and said in a somewhat shaky voice, "Florencita, look how strong these shoes are. They will last you for a long time."

Florence took the shoes and went to her room to think over the situation. She lay down on her cot and closed her eyes. She told herself a story about an orphan girl who grew up to be a princess. The prince in the story found a dainty black slipper in a hay stack. He said to himself that he would marry the girl who had a small enough foot to fit the slipper. He went around to all the farms looking for the girl of his dreams. He found the orphan girl milking cows in a barn and made her try it on. The shoe fit her dainty foot perfectly, so he took her away to be his princess. Florence fell asleep listening to the tune of the train whistle, singing its lonely song in the distance.

The next morning, Florence was up early and already dressed. She combed her short wavy hair and stared at the freckles on her face. She looked at her image in the small mirror her mother had given to her. She remembered asking her mother why she had spots on her face when no one else in the family had them. Her mother had told her that when she was born, she was so special, the stars came down from the sky and landed on her cheeks. Florence was satisfied with her mother's explanation and she felt good about her face.

Florence hurried into the kitchen where her mother was standing at the stove, stirring *atole* in a big pot. She had watched her mother, many times, mix blue corn meal with water. She cooked it until it became a thick cereal. Besides tasting good mixed with milk and sugar, her mother had said that *atole* was good for everything from colds to arthritis.

Florence was wearing a yellow dress which had been given to her by Mrs. Stremel. Mrs. Stremel had given her a bunch of old dresses that her daughter had outgrown. Florence picked one of the longer dresses that morning so the brown boots would be somewhat hidden. She had already accepted the idea of wearing the shoes to school. All of a sudden, school had become important because now she would learn to read books. Books would open up the world to her.

Joe came into the kitchen and said, "Let's go *manita*. Today I will walk with you and show you the way."

Mrs. Torres handed Florence a burrito wrapped in paper, kissed her and waved good-by at the screen door.

"*Adiós, Hijos,*" she said as she made a big sign of the cross in the air, giving them her blessing. She watched the two walk down the dusty path to the main dirt road which led to the school.

The school was a mile away near the town. As they passed each farm, a steady stream of children joined the parade. The children did not talk to Florence or Joe but whispered to each other and pointed fingers at them. Florence wondered why they were pointing but centered her thoughts on the magic of learning.

They finally approached the school. A young woman was standing outside greeting the children. She must be the teacher, Florence thought; and later on that day, she found out that her name was Mrs. Burger and she did not have any kids. Florence was a little bit apprehensive when Joe left her at school, but she occupied herself with watching the other kids and imitating them. Mrs. Burger led the children into the school. Florence followed into a big room where there was a huge blackboard with white markings on it. There were some nice chairs with little tables on top. There were more children than chairs so Florence had to sit on the floor. She watched and listened with all her might. She even succeeded in drawing some of the lines from the blackboard on the paper Mrs. Burger had given to her.

A bell rang and all the kids got up and left. Florence thought it must be time to go home, so she got up and followed the crowd. When she got outside, Florence started walking towards the road home. Mrs. Burger yelled her name and motioned her back to the school yard. She saw the kids eating and she realized it must be lunch time. She remembered the burrito her mother had packed. She took it out of her pocket and started to eat it. She was standing by herself, leaning against the school building. A pretty girl dressed in fine clothes came and stood in

76 • Magdalena Gallegos

front of her. Florence smiled at the girl and said hello. The girl looked suspiciously at the rolled up tortilla. Then she spotted Florence's shoes. She pointed at Florence and said something to the other girls that Florence did not understand. They all started laughing and pointing at Florence. Florence knew they were making fun of her and her shoes. She wanted to run and hide. The teacher came out and rounded up the children. She herded them back into the school. It seemed like hours till the bell rang to go home.

As soon as Florence got out of the door, she started to run. She didn't stop until she got home. By then she was breathing so hard that her chest felt like it was on fire. She sat down next to the kitchen door and took off the shoes. She crossed her arms and was determined not to let that day get her down. But it hurt so bad to think that there were people in the world who were cruel and unfriendly. And why did they keep calling her "Mexican." Her name was Florence. She was contemplating all this when her mother came out of the kitchen.

"Florencita, I didn't know you were home already. Why are you so quiet?"

"*Mamá. No me gusta la escuela.* I don't like school."

"*Porqué no te gusta, Hija.* Why don't you like school Florencita?"

"*Mamá,* the kids made fun of my burrito, they made fun of my shoes, and they kept calling me Mexican.

Florence's mother gathered her in her arms and said, "*Hija,* I will fix it."

With a determined look on her face, Mrs. Torres grabbed up the shoes and took them in the house. When the boys got home that afternoon, Mrs. Torres handed Joe the box with the shoes and told him to take them back to the store. They argued for a few minutes and Joe huffed off down the road leaving a dust storm behind him.

It was getting dark when Joe got back. He had another box under his arm. He also had a funny grin on his face. He handed Florence the box and told her to open it. She hesitated, but finally she lifted the lid. She stared into the box. Then, her whole face lit up and she started to yell, "*Mira, mira, mira es un milagro.*"

She lifted the black shiny shoes, with rows of tiny straps, out of the box and danced around the kitchen hugging them in her arms.

Not too much changed the next day except for her shoes. She was still the same person and she ate another burrito. She smiled at everyone and soon made friends. In time, some of the kids even wanted to trade their lunches for her burritos after they discovered how delicious they were. At night, when she got home from school, Florence would carefully take off the shiny black shoes, clean them with a little rag and put them on her bed, next to her pillow. She slept with them close to her as she slipped into her dreams.

Florence was still flying around in her dreams. It was so easy to fly. In fact, it was just as easy to fly in shiny black shoes as it was to fly barefoot.

TOÑO

César A. González

It was late August, 1955, almost thirty years ago. I remember that we were preparing to register students for the fall semester. I know I had my back to the faculty dining room windows because I remember looking over to my left at the principal gesturing discreetly to Carlos, the houseman, to come over. We had just started lunch and were listening to some announcements being read.

Don Alfonso, a kind but proper Stoneyhurst-educated man, sat his short, full body to the front of his chair at the head of the table. Among ourselves we sometimes called him Tata Poncho. He looked over his round steel-rimmed glasses at Carlos and whispered carefully. He had a way of working his mouth in exaggerated articulation, as though otherwise his listener might not understand. The white of his back teeth flashed every so often. Carlos leaned sideways, nodding his young old-with-work face. His black mustache spread to a smile, and he looked over Don Alfonso's pink crowned pate toward the window. Something was going on behind me.

I didn't bother to look around. I couldn't have seen much anyway; the window panes were frosted glass. Only a couple of the heavy hand-welded central panels had been pulled to either side of the four rectangular windows that lined that side of the dining room. Outside there was a small overgrown oasis of a garden with some sad apple trees and alamos — a bit of green between the faculty residence and the desert worn adobe wall that separated us from the dusty grounds of the school.

The reading and the lunching went on. It was the main meal of the day. I had learned to get used to that. Mexico had inherited its eating hours from Spain — and that made sense. It was too hot in the desert to do much between noon and 3:00 p.m. anyway. I didn't like to take a nap after meals. I hated waking up thinking it was morning and then, with a time-space lag lurch, realize it was the afternoon of the day I thought was over.

The dining room noises were sharp, amplified. The entire house was tile floors and plaster over double hollow brick — sounds were exaggerated. Whenever a heavy-handled knife dropped onto one of the overlarge formica-topped dining room tables, it shot a blast of adrenalin up noses, and everyone brightened up, startled. Tata Poncho would lift off his chair. Once, someone dropped a full bottle of milk onto a table, and he stood straight up.

Carlos hurried smoothly and silently back into the room. He had a way of easing each heel down carefully as he moved quickly and deliberately about his work. He co-conspirited briefly with Don Alfonso and went on about serving the dozen or so of us men who shared the faculty house.

The reading ended, but before conversation could get started, Don Alfonso made a brief announcement. Some boys had been at the apple trees. Carlos had caught one. He was in one of the small front parlors. I was to take care of the matter. The young teachers and older staff approved, wondering what I would do. They were good people, and I enjoyed working with them. I had come there to teach, and to improve my Spanish. I was twenty-four and had been there a year. I was the Americano on the staff — a guest of sorts; just as I was always considered somehow Mexican in the States — an outsider of sorts. In

82 • César A. González

those days there was no such thing as a Chicano. You were either a Gringo, a Pocho, or worse.

Toño, I'm having a little trouble seeing your face. You were tall for an eleven year old, thin and poor. Your face was just a bit long and narrow — or was it your high forehead and the way you combed your hair back so that it stood up a bit. You didn't have any socks on.

The world was a good place to be then, and I had it all figured out. My academic isolation had shown me in its shelter that there was a plan and a reason and a logic to the universe. And if things weren't all they might be, I'd help to set the world right, and it would be spring again and warm mornings and fields of flowers everywhere. If everybody would just do the right thing and stop being selfish, we'd all be happy again.

Toño, you were a problem to be resolved that afternoon. I smiled and told you my name; your mouth went all full of cry. You sobbed in that little tile-floored echoing room that smelled like it had just been rag mopped — with its proper little table and spartan little chairs. You said something that I didn't understand, about getting food for your mother in the hospital, and you cried some more and looked skinny and lonely. Why hadn't you just walked out the front door when Carlos left you there to wait for me?

I asked you if you'd eaten. You shook your head no, and I said we'd have to do something about that. We both felt better outside walking around to the back of the house. The air was rich with the hot desert of northern Mexico. We went to the kitchen where there were after-meal smells and the clatter of clean up. The two old spinster sisters that cooked — I don't remember their names — said sure they could get a little bite together for a young man who hadn't eaten yet. They took you into the kitchen and said they'd call me when you were finished.

Later, we sat in the dusty school yard under an alamo, on one of the new benches bolted down on stubby cement cones. The cones reminded me of the *piloncillos* of hard brown sugar that I'd buy for my mom from José Solario, Prop., at La Esmeralda Market on the corner of 28th and Maple in Los Angeles. I was a dark and skinny and quiet little boy too.

You told me again that your mother was in the county hospital, that she didn't get enough to eat, that you were trying to get food for her. I couldn't believe you. But how could you make up a story like that? And just to explain why you'd taken one unripe apple? And yes, you were interested in going to school. (I'd talk to Tata Poncho about that later. Who knows what good thing might come from that apple — like the happy endings in the movies.) I'd keep in touch with you and see what I could do about your mom, remember?

You pointed to your house on the other side of the bridge that crossed the wide, dry boulder-bottomed river bed along the side of the school yard. From there, I remember how the river blundered its uneven way through downtown and north into the desert again. I gave you a few peso bills — they always seemed worn so soft in Mexico — and sent you on your way.

Dr. Berumen, the young doctor who taught anatomy and biology in the senior grades, went with me to the hospital. We found your mother in a ward for the incurables. She was lying on her side — legs and arms tucked into a clutched fetal position, glutinous black eyes staring out of dark sockets. She was a José Guadalupe Posada skeleton. Berumen told me that we had to get her to a private hospital. With an operation, chances were she might recover. I don't remember what her trouble was, but you remember, don't you? He'd take care of surgery and medications. I'd get some money together for the hospital bills. That wasn't a problem. After all, the best families sent their sons to us to be educated, and wealthy people from throughout the state had their sons on a waiting list to be admitted to our school. I was the smart young American teaching at the best school in town, and popular with the money people. I had more dinner invitations than I could handle. A few calls and visits would take care of the hospital bills. I'd see to that.

— But there was the matter of your father. After all, I couldn't just move in and take over. However, before the week was out the county clinic sent your mother home. The next day I went over the bridge to your home on the other side of town to see your father. It was mandatory to wear a coat and tie at all times. In the desert! It was expected. I was uncomfortable. The neighbors looked up at me from a distance.

84 • César A. González

They didn't say a word. They knew there was trouble at that home; something was happening.

Inside it was dark. The mattress looked thin and hard. I remember that the head of the bed was made of dark-colored tubing. (One of my first memories as a child of three on 28th Street is of a bed just like that, except that it was narrower.) I don't remember your father's face at all, nor how many children there were. I do remember that some of them were crying. I asked them, didn't they want their mother well again, up and walking, cooking and washing for them and doing the things that make home. Berumen arranged for an ambulance to take her the following day to a private hospital.

That day was also the first day of registration for the new school year, and we were all busy helping out in the front office. I was surprised when I was called to the phone; one of the cooks said that she had found the little boy who had eaten in the kitchen the other day, crying at the front door. You wouldn't talk to anyone, but you were asking for me.

Your mother had died that morning. I stood stunned, as though in the after-echo and din of a bell just done ringing. Damn it! That wasn't the way things were supposed to happen. Do you remember the details of that day, Toño? I asked you to come with me to Don Alfonso's office. I wanted to be excused from school.

I had just told him that your mother was dead, when you went pale, limp, and collapsed. You hadn't eaten properly for days.

I got you back to the cooks whose names I don't remember, told them not to give you too much too fast, and for Carlos to get you to a shower and into a bed.

Back at your home, your family and the neighbors had taken over and were preparing your mother properly for burial. Because of her disease — I still can't remember what it was — the law would not allow her to be buried from a church. However, she had to be buried within twenty-four hours.

I got some money together and added it to the amount I knew the neighbors had given to your father. (There's always somebody to take up a collection in a poor neighborhood. They did on 28th Street when my dad died in 1967.) I arranged for a priest to come to bless the body and meet us at the cemetery to bless the grave and say some prayers. We would bury her that same afternoon. I went back across the bridge to the faculty house and found you had taken your bath and were in bed. You looked weak, but I told you that no matter what, you were going to get up and get to your mother's funeral—even if I had to carry you. But first I wanted to get you some clothes.

You didn't have any socks and your shoes were dusty shreds. We went downtown to the best men's and boys' store in town—the one near the cathedral. We walked across the main plaza with its wrought iron gazebo in the middle and Porfirio Díaz benches for watching the girls on Saturday nights. I explained your situation privately to the storeowner and got a good discount. You got several complete outfits. After all, you'd need them in a couple of weeks when you started school on our side of the bridge.

I remember helping to carry your mother's coffin through the streets—men baring their heads and black-shawled women making the sign of the cross as we passed on our way to the cemetery outside of town. Some people followed—bare feet sandaled, shawls, click of rosary beads, salt traces of dried tears and sweat. It was all so new to me. I was sweating right through my suit coat. Don Alfonso said the coat was mandatory. It was expected. It was proper.

You looked uncomfortable by the graveside in your new clothes, standing there among your brothers and sisters. I don't think any of them had any socks on. Then there was the skeletal scatter and thump of earth thrown onto the coffin in the dry hole. That's the last thing I remember about that afternoon.

You did well in school. It was a big break for you, and you worked hard. I put you with one of our best sixth grade teachers—a bright, slightly matronly woman of about thirty. I just remember her last name. I opened an account for you at the book store. You got all your books and supplies free. I even got you a little canvas book carrier with real plastic straps. You looked just like one of the other boys at our school. And so you went back and forth across the bridge each day— from your home to our school and back again to the other side of town. Nobody in our school could have guessed where you came from.

One Thursday, about mid-November, the bright, slightly matronly sixth grade teacher informed me that you had not shown up in class that week. We got word to your home, somehow, and one of your older sisters came over the bridge to explain that the other kids in your neighborhood were making fun of you for going to the rich kids' school and dressing like a sissy. One of your brothers had just gotten out of the penitentiary and was giving you a bad time. You'd hopped a freight and had shown up at an uncle's home some five hundred miles to the south. I admired your courage, taking off like that, alone.

In a couple of weeks you were back in school, and a couple of weeks after that you were gone for good. I had tried. Later, I heard that you were working in a tortilleria just down the street.

One evening, toward the end of my third and last year in that town, I was standing in front of the school waiting to get across the street. It was a wide and busy avenue that formed a "Y" at that point — one part going northwest toward downtown and the cathedral, and the other northeast into an older but nice residential area away from the river. It was almost dark and the traffic was heavy. There was a momentary break in the traffic, and I stepped off the high curb. A boy dashed across the street and ran right into me.

Our eyes met in the dark, and all I could say was, "¡Toño!" Remember? I'd never seen you so happy. You were firming to a man. For their first time, I saw you laughing.

What's that, Toño? Why am I telling you all of this, thirty years later?

I thought you'd want to know.

I was trying to do the right thing.

I can what?

¡Toño!

VOLVER CON LA FRENTE MARCHITA

Ricardo Aguilar Melantzón

El acta de nacimiento que me dejó mi madre lee Rodolfo Belgrano Aúza, hijo de Rodolfo Belgrano Belgrano y Angela Aúza Cárdenas originarios de Ceballos, Coah. y residentes de Cd. Meoqui, Chih. Trabajo de secretario del Lic. Cipriano Revélez Acosta, jefe del despacho de abogados que lleva su nombre. Mi oficina queda en el edificio Sauer, frente al edificio de la aduana, sobre la 16 de septiembre, esquina con Avenida Juárez, noroeste del crucero, segundo piso, sobre la casa de cambio y expendio de lotería de don Máximo Regules y la zapatería Fornarina, al cruzar la calle del bar San Luis y a contraesquina del Banco Comercial.

—Anoche me agarré de la greña por enésima vez con la fiera, jefe. No se enoje, ya sé que van tres veces que llego tarde en la semana a los juzgados, y sí, si me he dado cuenta de la bola de tinterillos que zopilotean las oficinas de averiguaciones en busca de algún incauto o desesperado que les pida ayuda o sus servicios, no mi jefazo, no quiero ingresar a ese gremio. Si jefe, comprendo demasiado bien que usted se altere por mi comportamiento y que me regañe a cada rato, pues es bien importante que los casos se lleven a tiempo, aún cuando los clientes no sean ricos y poco podamos ayudarles en presentar una legítima defensa. No, no es necesario que me lo repita pues arrepentido de muchas cosas estoy de sobra. Si, ya sé que de ahí sale la papa para todos y que si no salimos todos al quite, conque falte uno se hunden los demás.

Pinche viejo tranza, como si el no llegara al despacho a las dos y toda la gente esperándolo con cara de uy uy uy y luego no se diera el lujo de hacerlos esperar otro rato mientras que se reporta con la joney para decirle no sé qué tantas cosas, que cómo estuviste buena anoche, que pronto nos vemos en el club para festejarla y continuarla, que al cabo aquí tengo un bola de gatos que me traigo cacheteando el pavimiento a cuarenta mil por hora y a mi antojo, que no te preocupes por lo de tu apartamento, que ya te compré unos muebles a todas emes y que la nueva tina yacuzzi es maravillosa con sus llaves doradas y su veneer imitación de mármol, que no, que no te puedes venir a trabajar a la oficina aunque te aburras de no hacer nada, que para eso te estoy manteniendo, además de que puede ser muy peligroso pues aquí circulan una bola de chismes gruesos y se puede dar cuenta la gorgona o nos pueden meter un chantaje y eso no y no se qué más.

—Si mi jefazo, no se preocupe que ahorita mismo salgo a sacar el expediente para que lo notarice y luego llevarlo a mil con el ministerio público. No, no habrá problemas con el juez pues ya lo tenemos tranzado y al cabrón del Cardenal tal vez hoy mismo le dicten acto de soltura. Sí, pobre desgraciado, ha pasado ya una semana de jueves en la jaula de los mandriles que es peor que el infierno pero tal vez con eso escarmiente y no se ande metiendo con las muchachas del Juait Leik aunque tampoco es seguro pues le encanta andar de mamacito.

—Ahi nos vemos mi jefazo, a la tarde platicamos otro rato.

Entro a mi cubículo, despacio, me siento, examino los zapatos todos raspados que compré en León el año pasado, me gustan mucho por la piel fina, casi elástica, cuadrados de la punta, anchos para mover los dedos, los pantalones de lana a puntitos grises ya los tengo hace tres años y los prefiero en los días de frío cortante por la reuma en la rodilla que no deja de joderme la borrega, la corbata de moda, color vino con su pescado pintado a mano, difícil de amarrarse por lo ancha, el saquillo jolingo azul marino que uso siempre para ir más o menos formal, ya todo algo luído de tanto planche y planche pero con el cuento de que uno tiene que andar a la línea para que le respeten el pinchurriento titulito de Lic.

Desde anoche anduve perdido en el tiempo. No sabía si era miércoles, jueves o qué, ni la fecha tampoco. Con decirte que cada vez que me pongo así pierdo hasta la noción de quién soy. Es la mentada desesperación de no saber ni pa dónde jalar ante las presiones que se me vienen encima, una tras otra cuando bien me va y en pelota cuando es normal, eso sin pensar en que muchas veces me encuentro con la necesidad de complacer a todo mundo y no se puede. Pinche espejo, me tienes que enseñar las arrugas que me fastidian las esquinas jaladas de los ojos, que me surcan la frente y aparecen cada vez con más tesón por entre labios y mejillas. Me lo haces a diario y a veces más seguido, que ya la greña me queda como un decímetro por arriba de las cejas, que sólo me falta que se me caigan unas lonillas para que sea tonsura perfecta, desde los bigotes y las cejas hasta la corona posterior, como el abuelo, relumbrón por todos lados, sin canas en la cabeza, con excepción de una o dos que me salen por las patillas, los bigotes y las barbas ya rete salpicados de blanco y eso que apenas vamos en los treinta y cinco, es que deveras estoy muy corrido sin aceite, te lo juro que no tengo ganas de rasurarme, mil veces prefiero irme con los cuates a echarnos unas frías y platicar de los desmadres de antes, cuando andábamos sueltos y solteros y la cruda aún valía la pena, antes de entrar en este rollo de que tienes qué, si no te chingas o, como dijo el otro, si no te aclimatas te aclichingas, eso y la ruca, pinche espejo, ni siquiera sirves para guiarme la navaja, o será que esta chimustreta moderna, de doble filo y toda la cosa no sirve pa cortarme las barbas mestizas, siempre que me rasuro aquí me corto y luego ando por todos lados con un pedacito de papel del escusado colgando del cachete para parar el escándalo de sangre que sale como si deveras y aunque mucho aplastes para que pare, sale más, como si adrede y lo peor es que seguido repites por la prisa de que tienes que salir volando mano, además, es rete importante que no te vean sangrando pos van a decir que eres un ñetas que jalas como te rasuras. Conste que la "Gillete multiusos" de dos filos no me ayuda a resolver rollos gruesos jurídicos ni me vuelve más simpático, ni hago mejores tranzas a las de costumbre. Salgo del quite en las situaciones más imposibles y si no me la crees pues nomás ándate

VOLVER CON LA FRENTE MARCHITA • 91

un día pegadito a mí y verás. Eso sí, cabrón espejo, me enseñas lo que soy cada mañana, no me dejas que me alebreste por demás, no dejas de decirme que yo es yo y eso me gusta. Muy distinto a como siento por la noche cuando la fiera sale a pasear y tengo que estarme solo, agüitado, perdido ante el recuerdo de los momentos delicados del primerizo amor, de todas las veces que estuviste sin darte cuenta, sin sacarle al parche.

Qué raro, es la primera vez que deveras te fijas en este cuarto rupa, no, peor, que las ventanas están cuadradas de abajo, redondas de arriba y cruzadas de maderas y vidrios ondulados que hacen que la gente se vea distorsionada, mas larga de arriba que abajo y así y la luz que entra por allí y más en el verano, estalla sobre las cuatro paredes verdes y la puerta, pero verde claro de hace veinte años, cartografiada de goteras cafés y globos de pintura inflados hace tantos meses, ya reventados, dejaron caer hojaldras de pintura como hojas de pan dulce, otras las taparon debajo del espejo detrás del retrato de Benito Juárez. A un lado de la silla y del armario, enfrente, alcanzas a divisar la reja de la aduana, rococó, llena de garigoleos, fierro negro volteado y torcido donde se paran la bola de viejos gordos, canosos, pelones, que se dedican a engañar al prójimo, a sacarle los pocos dineritos que tanto le ha costado juntar, para que no pase por allí ninguna cháchara sin pagar el impuesto debido que es propiedad de la nación, que todo ciudadano debe pagar para que el sistema continue operando pero que también sirve cantidad para que ellos se roben chingos de feria que les habrá de servir para establecerse como grandes señorones, para construirse sus casonas de millonada en los mejores barrios, para mandar a sus furris hijos a cultivarse al extranjero y convertirse en dignos representantes de sus padres, en nuevas sanguijuelas, burócratas perfectos. Alcanzas a divisar la hoja de vidrio doble giratorio sostenida de gigantes visagras, se abre y se cierra sin cesar, deja pasar a la mole de transeúntes que entran y salen a toda hora y con cada vuelta hecha un chispazo de luz que te pega sobre el vidrio de los lentes, bifocales, que te ayudan a existir.

¿Quién fué el que to platicó aquello de la aduana? ¿Qué querría decirte con eso? Tal vez jamás lo sepas pues nunca lo volviste a ver. Te examinas de nuevo ante el espejo, ante la luz naranja ya, ante un ruido callejero distinto al la refocilata de los carros de hace unos momentos. Te estrañas, volteas y sientes que algo sucede, no acabas de entender, te sorprende encontrar sobre la repisa del espejo una navaja de hoja, de las que siempre te han fascinado pero nunca has podido manejar por miedo a rasgarte la yugular. Todavía está lleno de grumos mojados de jabón llenos de pelitos, sin reconocerlos y eso que te acabas de afeitar, ya perdiste el mango de la sartén. Te duele el moño de seda apretada alrededor del cuello duro, prendido a la camisa con broches dorados, uno al frente, otro detrás y dos de lado, las puntas volteadas hacia afuera, de mariposa, que hacen juego con los ángulos de la corbata, en lugar de la mancha de mostaza del pantalón gris hay una raya bien planchada sobre el pantalón negro de tu traje de levita, desconocido, bien cortado, cómodo, que te perturba. Con la mano izquierda que luce anillo extraño de piedra verde junto al negro lunar de tu familia, te tomas el saco por las solaponas, lo abres, forro de seda china azul cielo, tres bolsitas, una bajo la otra a la derecha y una grande a la izquierda, debajo un chaleco gris a rayas, cadenita de oro trenzado a la florentina metida en la bolsita de lado izquierdo inferior donde tientas un reloj, lo revisas con detenimiento, como si descubrieras a alguien más, ya perdiste la urgencia, las preocupaciones que te llevaron a parate aquí, de repente ya no sabes de quién es ese relojazo, carátula de concha nácar y numeración marfil alrededor de una pequeña Terpsícore pintada a mano. Te tientas la extraña partidura a media cabeza, pero la sientes natural, no como cuando trataste de cambiar la forma de peinarte y sentiste que el pelo te dolía, los bigotes, la barba afeitada con pomada gruesa, perfumada, te fastidian, no te acostumbras a la comezón. Tras el reflejo, divisas el cuadro a un lado de la ventana, ya no el prieto rostro de Juárez sino otro enmarcado de blanco, severo, intransigente, poderoso y altivo, Don Porfirio. La silla, el armatoste de madera, de los que el ejército gabacho desechó después de la guerra de Corea, ahora elegante butaca de cuero, altas espaldas, gruesa colchonadura. Sigues estudiando de la reja, el edificio de ladrillo rojo, la luz sigue pegando en el espejo pero destella, la puerta cerrada. Te fijas en el marco de la ventana, diferente, rodeado de un paño color rojo, inunda de color tu elegante despacho. Escuchas ruidos extraños, bufidos de animal, tienes que asomarte a la ventana, quieres caminar, descubrir lo que afuera pasa pero no puedes, te quedas clavado, ahora reconoces que estás muerto de miedo, de la impresión ya te curaste de la cruda, estás prendido al suelo a diez uñas, miras, quieres saber a qué se debe, sientes muy agusto, los pies enfundados, casi guantes de ternera, botines altos apretados, amarrados, cintas largas que entrelazan multitudes de agujeros repetidos de empeine a calva. Te recobras un poco, sueltas la loción agarrada en la derecha desde que entraste, das vuelta, caminas hacia el sol, los ruidos van creciendo, la gente se arremolina abajo, sientes mucho apuro, por fin te asomas. Las calles atiborradas, de aquí para allá pasean los oficiales en sus caballos, extraordinariamente elegantes, seda azul marino realzada de dorados, charreteras, galones, medallas, sables, botones, rayas rojas sobre las costuras del pantalón y cascos kaiserianos de acero bruñido y oro completan el ajuar, contraste de plumas blancas de remate y monturas negras. Toda la gente, todas las clases, las que no tuvieron que atender designios de patrones, patronas, se han escapado, buscan guarecerse en algún lugar propicio donde puedan observar sin que los corran o molesten, los señores bajo sombreros de paja, señoras cubiertas de pañoleta, faldas anchas, las mayorías, hacen resaltar a damas ricas de largos chiffones, sombreros de ala, velo y parasoles.

La calle viste de gala, pilares de madera, labrados, pintados de blanco rematados de capiteles cabezados a la griega, entre cada columna enormes paños extendidos en orlas, los colores patrios sobre ventanas de los edificios, por fin sabes por qué la luz rojo sangre te llenó el espejo. Ocurre algo importante, no estás ahí al azar, tienes que bajar ahora mismo. A fuerza de costumbre ajena caminas al rincón, tomas bastón, puño cabeza de águila real que te recuerda imágenes encontradas en retratos de ruinas aztecas, abres la puerta, te colocas el bombín. El sol aturde los sentidos, ciega tanto que hiela unos instantes, la gente se apelotona, empuja, parece que se va a presentar un merolico, a la orilla de banquetas de madera, vuela un aire a sudor matizado de perfume barato, una marcha de John Phillip Souza, aturde el chasquido de los címbalos, los redobles, xilófonos, cornetas, hacen temblar el cuero, pasa la banda de guerra, detrás levanta polvo un pelotón de infantería, las puntas de las banderas truenan contra el viento, por sobre taconazos y rechinidos de banqueta y escalera oyes el "Flancuizquieeeerdo . . . ya!" Divisas para el norte, allá lejos, distingues las cabezas de cuatro azabaches, peinados remilgosamente en trensas y listones blancos, dentro de la carreta oscura figuran los rostros, las manos, blancas, prietas, dos ancianos, cerca, te das cuenta, como en las lecciones de historia, Porfirio Díaz acompañado de William Howard Taft.

Llegas jadeante, entras por la puerta oeste, sacas la cartera, un papel amarillo, doblado, mal metido, rueda por el suelo, se agacha el guardia, lo recoge, lo devuelve, te identificas con las credenciales que

94 • Ricardo Aguilar Melantzón

allí encuentras, acomodas el telegrama, pasas. Te reciben bien, como personaje importante, allegado a los grandes intereses nacionales. En el salón central de la aduana, bajo capiteles de acero pintado, columnas, fustes de mármol italiano blanco y contrabases del mismo rosa, techo de plachas labradas en madera y recubiertas de hoja de oro, entre pinacoteca de José María Velasco y otros paisajistas mexicanos, por exóticas alfombras y mármoles pulidos se congrega ya la exaltada concurrencia, alguien se te acerca,

—Ramiro, ¿cómo estás?, qué bueno que viniste pues ya sabes, de esto depende que sigamos como hasta ahora . . . .

Lo saludas, le dices que no te sientes bien y te retiras hacia un rincón. Pasan adelante el presidente y su invitado, roto el murmullo, estallan los aplausos, se cierne el silencio a la expectativa de las proclamaciones, el viejo oaxaqueño, alto, parece chiquito frente a la mole americana, inaugura la entrevista, agradece la asistencia del sajón y pronostica labores éxitosas, el gringo habla de jouspitelided, mui bounitou y otras. Sigue el brindis, termina la ceremonia.

Una sala estilo Deco da ventanas a la calle, la sala azul, descansan en sillones, mullidos de terciopelo azul rey, bajo la resolana del zaguán, los próceres. La pesadez del blanco obliga a que respire fuertemente, retumba el resuello animalesco por todas partes, el traje gris de casimir inglés ya muestra arrugas cansadas en la ingle, corvas y codos, contrasta fuertemente con el general mexicano, puritano ante el uniforme de gala cortado a la francesa, casi negro, cuello y puños bordados de olivo plata y oro, dobles franja roja de canto en cada pierna, medallas, estrellas y reconocimientos obtenidos en aras de marciano heroísmo el 2 de abril y después, galardones nacionales, extranjeros, La Croix de Guerre, El Aguila Azteca, El Sol del Plata, The Cross of Saint Stephen, La Cruz de Hierro y más prendidas bajo les favoris pommadés a la Kaiser, o mejor la soi même y un kepís de Marechal de Champ 'a la Belle Epoche', hoja de oro, charol y todo, las voces se suceden, una fuerte tirando a ladino, otra gruesa, pausada pero al temple, evidente que ambos saben su negocio, luego se notan los estilos como en pelea de gallos.

Sales de la sala central con parte de la concurrencia, despistado, confundido ante lo que has presenciado, en vez de salir por la puerta principal te regresas por donde entraste pero te pierdes, en vez de tomar la primera vidriera vas a la segunda, no se nota, abres e inmediatamente te das cuenta de lo que acabas de hacer, estás en el foyer al salón de la entrevista, nadie se fija, todos muy atentos, te quedas unos momentos, no te la quieres perder . . .

T:

Pueis sei mai fren Doun Porfiriou, nueistrou neicioun teiner miuchous proubleimas now with the Kaiser Wilhelm. El creier quei nousoutrous nou eistar seirious dei eintrar ein güerra coun the Axis sei lous eileimaneis nou reispeitar soubeiraneias dei lous neiciouneis-amigous dei Iuroupa. Coumou iusteid sabeir, lous Eistadous Iunidous coumproumeiteirsei coun treitedous internaeiciounaleis pour deifen-deir el libeirteth dei eisous neiciouneis and if lous eileimaneis eintrar in güerra, nousoutrous eintrar too because we are miuchou coum-proumeiteedous and teiner entereiseis miuchou fiuerteis to protect.

D:

Berri gud mai dir Presidente Teft, Mécsicou iss mach afrei off guar tu-also pero Mécsicou jevin big problens gardin his releicions güit Jérmani tu. Güi nid dyur góbermen tu guib Mécsicou una oportiúniti tu démostrei jis gud vólunti. Di jístori prub det Mécsicou ebri taim jeb guib jis jel tu di Iunaites Steis bat neber jeb ricib natin bec fron det cantri. Güi nid tu spik in ril guors abau Mécsicou interes tu.

T:

Jablar deireichou mister Presidentei, seir miuchou empourtantei teiner good idea dei quei Mécsicou quierer.

D:

Mécsicou nid tu ricober litol det it jes los tu di Iunaites Steis en di guorl. Ji nid tu queptiur jis los aidentiti neshionel.

T:

Pueis Eistadous Iunidous sabeir quei Mexicou teiner miuchou grandei friendship coun Kaiser Wilhelm and that the Kaiser jabeir teineedou miuches paleivbras coun iústeid. Eistadous Iunidous queirer teiner más grandei friendship coun Mexicou quei Mexicou coun Elei-meinia, queirer start up talks soubrei inteirquembious coummercialeis and other reileishiouneis coun our dear neighbor al sour, peirou tem-biein deiber deicir to Mexicou quei Eistadous Iunidous seir miuchou malou enemigou when provoked.

D:

¡Mister Présiden!, ai güil no permit di invit person in mai jaus, iben de présiden of di Iunaites Steis, tu spik abau mai cantri in dos gours. Mécsicou is di sóberei neicion. Güi jev grei prai en poğüer, grei

96 • Ricardo Aguilar Melantzón

frens en elais. If dyiu inten tu spik to as es icuals güi güil lissen bat du nat meik trets hir.

T:

Darmei miuchou lastimou quei Mister President Deeaz piensar this way. Nousoutrous nou quierer ensiultar a niueistrou good friend and neighbor peirou tiener infourmeis quei deicir that the Mexican government jabeir tranzadou coun el Kaiser Wilhelm and nousoutrous quierer risoulveir eistou grandei proubleima because if Eistadous Iunidous eintrar in güerra coun Eleimania poudi seir miuchou deeficil tu countiniu dei ser emigou dei Mexicou if Mexicou permaneiceir niutral.

D:

Berri gud mai fren, güi agri guan ting, güi disagri . . .

de pronto alguien estornuda, algo cae, pesado rueda por el suelo, muchos se lanzan a cogerlo, otros corren, cierran el paso, se investigará el incidente, encuentran una Derringer cargada, dos tiros, como la de Mimí Blanchetour, alguno la metió a pesar del cateo, no te extraña pues acabas de entrar y nadie te registró, pronto salen los personajes escoltados, el estado mayor da instrucciones:

—"¡Que nadie salga!, que todo mundo se vacíe las bolsas, cateo general!" Respiras, sabes que estás a salvo, traes los documentos, te vacías las bolsas, te catean, una caja de cerillos, dos habanos, el telegrama, la cartera, unas monedas, tres botones de repuesto y el anillo, sorprendido ni sabías lo que traías, te llama el oficial, te pide la cartera, la inspecciona quisquilloso, parece satisfecho, te mira a los ojos, desdobla el telegrama, lo revisa, lo notas nervioso, te sigue examinando de reojo, revisa lo demás, devuelve todo menos el papel amarillo, adelante, registra a otro, veloz, empiezas a pensar, ¿Qué dirá el documento? Si me quieren arrestar qué voy a hacer? ¿Por dónde me escapo? ¿Qué me va a suceder? ¿Cómo me safo? A la salida te detiene el coronel, ya dio orden de aprensión y el sargento te saca del brazo, detrás marchan cuatro, entran a otra sala, la jefatura provisional del regimiento, ordenan que te sientes frente al escritorio, todos callados, te sudan las manos, te muerdes las uñas, ¿eres el único detenido? El oficial cierra las puertas, te pregunta que si quién eres, a qué te dedicas, dónde vives, quién te invitó, puedes darle nombres de personas conocidas que puedan atestiguar tu declaración, no sabes qué hacer, si le dices la verdad no te va a creer, mientes, dices que si quieren pueden cruzar la calle a tu despacho, que allí hay quién puede dar parte, sabes que esto no va a ninguna parte, lo único que puede ocurrirte es un milagro, mientras no sepas qué te pasa tampoco puedes regresar, crees que el coronel quiere creerte, te acusa de connato de atentado, que el cargo no se ha formalizado pero que las circunstancias apuntan hacia tí, el delito es grave, te muestra el telegrama, pide que expliques lo escrito en alemán, abajo aparece la firma "Zimmerman", dices lo primero que se te ocurre, tratas importaciones y exportaciones con intereses extranjeros, tienes que ver con personas que no saben español, seguido se comunican en su lengua y tienes que hacerlo traducir para hacer los tratos, el coronel sigue frunciendo el seño, no se convence, le dices que pasen al despacho que allí encontraran documentos similares con fecha previa, se aclarará el asunto, decide por fin, llama al sargento.

"Llévelo escoltado, revise todo y tráigame las pruebas."

Pisas el primer escalón que sube a los altos, vienen bajando, sin deberla ni temerla, unas gentes, automáticamente te haces a un lado, pasan, se disculpan, discurres furiosamente, los soldados también esperan a que pasen, saltas, llegas arriba, te gritan, corres espavorido, la puerta, no traes la llave, abres de fuerte puntapié, entras, pertrechas con escritorio, silla y armario, quieres ahogar los gritos desaforados de los que golpean, los muebles se deslizan hacia atrás, una mano empuñada de revólver Colt 45 se entremete por la rendija, quieres prensar los muebles, no escuchas el tronido, como si fueras otro ves la chispa, sientes caer, nada te duele, sólo tientas mojado y un suave latido bajo la axila izquierda.

Sobre la repisa del espejo, me guiña un ojo el filo doble de la "Gillete multiusos" y el paradeo abre y cierra de la puerta de la aduana, bonito caso les toca resolver a estos pendejos, el humo de la Colt se levanta por un lado de la punta cuadrada del zapato.

THE HOUSEKEEPER

Ronnie Burk

Ricki rang the doorbell to the enormous carved door of ornate lion heads. The lady of the house was not in. The housekeeper answered the door. A whiff of beans simmering on the stove permeated the atmosphere which was congenial enough. I immediately adored the housekeeper, her dark indian complexion, barefoot in a cotton dress. "Excuse the house. The kitchen is such a mess but the workmen haven't come in this week to finish." She rolls her eyes heavenward. All conversation is conducted in the most accomodating of Spanish. She excuses herself and heads back to the television set which is just now switched to the Mexico City version of The Dating Game starring some moustachioed caballero and three not so lucky ladies. Everyone goes about their business. Ricki and Miguel dash for the swimming pool, the house keeper sits before the t.v., I am to make the most of it. Hungry, I head for the refrigerator, decide on matzos, creamcheese and herring. I haven't eaten all day and my body was rattling from too much coffee.

"I just put the beans on they won't be done till this afternoon." The kitchen is stripped down to plywood and sheet rock. Everything, herbs, spices, pots and pans, cannisters of flour and rice and beans, everything is in the dining room. Only the beans in the earthenware jarro sitting on the orange glowing burner of the electric stove made the kitchen. I adjourn to the frontroom with my plate of herring and matzos. "There's coffee if you'd like." The housekeeper calls from her chair. "Oh no." I answer, "water is fine." Pouring water into a champagne glass. I pick up a magazine and read Playgirl's interview with Paul Krassner which entertains me for about 12 minutes, that, and lunch.

Fumbling thru the house, huge and monstrous, the underbelly of some extravagant dynastic dragon. Full of mirrors and marble and chandeliers and even a white grand piano just to let you know. They are boxes of books all about and I am determined to read for the hour. Can't find anything to read till I discover Georgia O'Keefe's BOOK OF PAINTINGS. She narrates. I take in chaos of house. Decide I would rather sit in t.v. room amid boxes, shelves, television show, warmth and hospitality of housekeeper than lonely front room. I like Georgia O'Keefe's voice on the page. Painting and her life, the psychic biography of the artist, the streets of New York or the desert in bloom. Turning from page to page I felt the book was a picture of my own experience. The painter even talks about her days in Texas. The housekeeper interrupts my reverie with her giggling at the suggestive language the contestants are using back and forth. I look up from the book and set it aside. "These games are so silly. Do you think you could go on t.v. and say such things?" I smile and shake my head. "ME EITHER!" she says emphatically. Turning her full attention towards me she asks in a softer tone, "Are you from Laredo?" "No, I'm not. I'm from San Antonio." "I use to live in San Antonio, for 3 years I lived in San Antonio. My daughter still lives in San Antonio. Do you like San Antonio?" "Yes I do. It's close to my family and I have friends there." She looks back at me intently, "Well I was never happy there. I worry about my daughter she studies there now but I just don't like her being there. There's so much drugs and crime and she is young and easily influenced." I want to drop my mouth open but instead I find myself nodding in agreement.

100 • Ronnie Burk

"Yes, it's true. I wouldn't want to deny that about the United States. There is alot of drug use and crime amongst the youth."

"And then there is Immigration. I am always worried she or my sons will be harassed by them."

"I get carded everyonce and awhile in San Antonio." I tell her.

She shakes her head. "It's dangerous. So many people get killed crossing the border."

"And are you from Nuevo Laredo?" I ask her.

"Oh No! I'm from Coahuila. I live on a small ranch outside of Torreon. My husband and I have land and we work it. Now and then I come to Nuevo Laredo to visit a sister of mine and sometimes I work when I find it and can cross over. Immigration has made it even more difficult to cross and they follow no real policy. It's just whoever they let cross over. One woman may get to go and the next one won't, even if they have the same papers and the same reason.

"You're talking about the Mexican Immigration?"

"Yes. I wish my two sons who live in Houston and my daughter would come home. My two sons work and make good money in Houston. Sometimes they send the money home. But I tell them the money's no good. Dollars have to be converted into pesos and what can you buy with pesos? Better I tell them if they would just come back to the ranch and help their father work the ranch. I love it. We have a few cows and goats and chickens and grow corn and beans and I have my own garden, squash, tomatoes, chilis. We have just everything and if they would just come home it would set my mind to ease. Times are getting harder. So many people just pass thru just looking for food. We were lucky this year. We had rain. Further south there was a drought. We'll be okay this year. With corn and beans what more do you need?"

She looked at me as she gestured with her hand to underline her question. Her voice echoed through everything I knew. What more do you need? Transistor radios, tapes and tape decks, beer and topless bars, fiber-glass cars and plastic ersatz food cooked in micro-wave ovens. Her children caught up in the great American past time of consume, consume, consume. And in Houston, the city I have learned to hate the most. Can even take Denver over Houston, anything over Houston. My madness in Houston. Houston the petrochemical post-technocratic boom town bursting at the seams. Thick with racial violence and police brutality. Right Wing Depot of Miller's AIR CONDITIONED NIGHTMARE. Swelling with a generation of Mexican's,

THE HOUSEKEEPER • 101

Vietnamese, Haitians, Yankees, Texans, Chicanos, everybody checking into the Hotel Futurama. Good GAWD Houston breakdown. The freeways collapsing as they build them. Obsolete before they open them. My only retreat in the city, The Rothko Chapel. That, and the amiable funky mansion Lynn Randolph works in. Her canvas's stuck amongst the antique furniture. Upstairs in her studio getting the light of twilight down on canvas. Lynn always made a visit to Houston a joy, but that was just about it.

Lady, your children may never come home. It may be your grandchildren who will seek you out. After a life of hamburgers and the Astrodome. Yes, what more do you need? Beans and corn. The mountains to one side, the wet (mexican) earth beneath your feet tending to a garden of tomato plants. All this floods thru my thoughts in a matter of seconds I look into her face and answer her question. "Nothing." We agree the world is getting tough, television is dumb. Clean air is better than central heating and air-conditioning. The life of the planet is at stake.

Oh, how I love her and her beans on the electric stove. Her combed hair neatly braided. Her gold earrings. Her soft voice with all of it's inflection. My first impulse was to stand and bow to her the way the Zen masters teach you to bow before a dignified and respected being. But realize this would be too weird, too incongrous to her own simplicity. She reaches into her lap as if she were picking up a flower but it is a small comic book. A copy of The Miracles of The Virgen Of San Juan. Entertaining herself, as any Hindu would, with the divine, she lights a cigarette and offers me one. We smoke together as Ricki walks back in from the pool. Dripping wet, her black eye make-up running down the sides of her face. My friend and I, who know so much and yet know so little.

"I'm sorry to keep you. You must be getting bored."

"Bored? Oh no, not at all. In fact I have been having this incredible conversation with this woman." The housekeeper looks at the both of us. How absurd we must appear to her. She has the very peace and contentment some of us will travel around the world to find. Only to discover you can go around the world but you can never get any further than your own heart. It has been more than an hour and now it's time for us to go grocery shopping. I bid farewell to the housekeeper as she walks us back towards the huge ornate door, and thank her for her hospitality and graciousness.

HIS MOTHER'S IMAGE

Manuel Ramos

Tony de la Vida died in Vietnam when he was twenty. A bullet from a high powered automatic weapon tore out most of his intestines and stomach. At the instant of his death, as his blood flowed into the dark, damp earth of the jungle, the ghost of his grandfather walked up to him, cradled his head and whispered in Spanish. The apparition had tears in its eyes but Tony noticed that it was smiling too. He remembered the toothy grin. For Tony, dying confirmed that he had seen *la llorona* one summer night twelve years before.

Tony's death was one of many that day, uncomplicated by terror or prolonged suffering. It went unnoticed except by the remnants of Tony's family, spread across the Southwest, and by his friends back home in Florence.

Florence was, and still is, a small town of three thousand people. It sits near the Arkansas River, twenty minutes from Canon City. The people of Florence described where they lived in relation to other places like Canon City, or thirty miles from Pueblo or, when the listener knew little of Colorado, "a couple of hundred miles south of Denver." That is how it was in Florence. Life was compared to something else, some other way.

Tony was raised by the people he called his grandparents in a large stone house. It had two stories, a dilapidated garage, a chicken coop, two dog houses, and an apple tree. Chickens and dogs roamed in the back. The grandmother, Jesusita, was boss as she gathered eggs and threw feed to the hens. Kids trailed after her or chased the animals. There were always kids.

Jesusita and her husband Adolfo raised more than a dozen children. Some were their own but the others, Tony never learned how many, were given to the couple to care for without any formal adoption process or the interference of a social services agency. These children were cast-offs. Orphans and abandoned children like Tony found a family at the house of Jesusita and Adolfo Gonzales.

Tony's *abuelito* was a storyteller, a man who related his history and the history of his family in long talking sessions that fascinated the children.

Adolfo liked for the kids to sit with him at the table at night while he drank Jim Beam and Coca-Cola. He talked of his life or the lives of his brothers in Mexico and the States since he had come north looking for work after Villa stopped fighting. Adolfo's voice boomed across the room in a rhapsodic mixture of Spanish and English that flowed with poetry, curses, songs and other sounds the children did not understand but which always fit into the story at the right time. Adolfo told a different story each time or added to one he had told before. The updates changed the meaning completely but they made absolute sense to the kids.

Tony would sit with a glass of coke listening to Adolfo. The boy took a drink from his glass each time the grandfather sipped the bourbon. In this way Tony learned of the Mexican revolution, of working on the farms and of the spirits of the men who had died in the mines of Chandler on the outskirts of Florence.

The stories continued through the years. Adolfo died when Tony was fourteen, surrounded by his children, in the hospital that was a converted chicken farm. On his last night he began the story of a card game with the devil but he did not finish.

When Tony was eight he went for the first time to the river with his brother Johnny and some of his buddies.

It was a hot, dry summer. Jesusita allowed him to go with Johnny to the river to escape the heat. The boys swam in the river where a pool had formed that was deep and still. Trees kept the place hidden from anyone on the highway that followed the river for a short span outside the town. The river was wide and fast and perfect for tubing and fishing. The boys swam most of the time or shot at the birds with their BB guns.

Tony floated for hours in the water almost forgotten by the older ones. The water was cool and Tony soaked away thoughts of his missing mother. He wondered who she was, why she had left him. He imagined what she looked like.

On one of the days that stretched for miles across the cloudless sky, Tony first encountered *la llorona*. He was at the river, floating in the water listening to the *chicharras*. Johnny and Paco were by the bank, smoking and talking about Linda Garcia and her dark, almost black nipples.

Tony was drifting, half asleep, when he noticed the change. The *chicharras* quit their humming. Birds suddenly flew from the trees in squawking bunches. Tony opened his eyes to see what was causing the commotion but the brightness of the sun blinded him and he saw only a glare from the water.

Then there was silence. It covered the woods like a thick, heavy blanket. Tony swam to the shore.

He quickly put on his clothes. The sun was still out, the day hot, but Tony shivered in the silence. He did not hear Johnny or Paco. No wind stirred the wild grass. The roar of the river was different. It was muffled and seemed to come from far away.

Suddenly there was a moan from the river, a noise Tony would remember for the rest of his life. The sad, melancholy cry surrounded him. It created feelings that he did not understand. Tony's eyes watered, filled with tears, and he was forced to wipe them. The sound was of a woman crying. She wanted something so bad it was killing her not to have it. Tony looked up and down the river but saw nothing.

Johnny and Paco found him at the river's edge, crying softly that he wanted to help her. They had heard the sound too. Johnny said it was *la llorona*, the woman who cries, and it was time to go home.

As they walked away, Tony looked back at the river and saw a woman dressed in black wandering along the bank.

That night Adolfo told Tony the story of *la llorona*. "*Hijo*," he began, "*la llorona* is a woman condemned by God himself to roam the earth searching for her children, children she threw away years ago."

He held his glass of liquor with small, bony hands. The veins in his arms popped out of his skin. Their gray color deepened to blue as he drank more Jim Beam. His hair was thin and white, his moustache full and gray. Two gold teeth glistened from the corner of a smile that stretched from his black moist eyes to the wrinkled, grizzled chin.

Jesusita hollered at him from the kitchen where she stirred a pot of beans. "*Viejo, dejalo*. These things are not for children. *Mira, nomás*. You will make him afraid to go to sleep, afraid of his own shadow."

Her words were wasted. Both the boy and the old man were determined that the story would be told.

The woman was a young Mexican from South Texas. Adolfo was not sure if she was rich or poor but he was positive that she was beautiful with Indian looks framed by long, rich black hair. She was desired by every man in her *pueblo*, but she wanted only one—Don Antonio Perez, a rancher and a *vaquero*. She snared him, of course, and they were said to be more in love than two people have a right to expect. They prospered in wealth, influence, and happiness. After a few years of marriage the woman gave birth to three children in rapid succession, two boys and a girl that mirrored her beautiful mother.

That was where the love story went awry. Don Antonio loved the children with a generosity that bordered on the hysterical. He showered the babies with gifts they could not use for years. Toy horses, guns, clothes and money piled up in their rooms. He watched over them with a single-mindedness that caused him to neglect his business. He gave them so much love that he had little left for his wife. He loved her, but not with the same intensity of his love for the children.

Jealousy replaced the feelings of affection the wife held for her family. She blamed the children for the lack of fire in her husband's lovemaking. She saw them as rivals for his attention. When she remembered the love from the early days of her marriage to Don Antonio she hated the children more for taking it away.

106 • Manuel Ramos

She made a plan to do away with the children so that Don Antonio would love her again. She turned to the devil and his ways for help.

"*Pues, tu sabes, 'jito,* that in those days it was much easier to deal with the devil than it is now. *Brujas* were everywhere. A person only had to ask the right one to get what he wanted. That's what a person had to do." The old man whispered the word *bruja* each time he said it, making it sound sinister and threatening.

"The woman sought the help of one of the bad *brujas*. The *bruja* told her to take the children to the river where the devil would trade Don Antonio's love for the little ones. On the night of the exchange, driven by hatred, she threw them into the rushing water."

Tony drank the last of his Coca-Cola and tried not to think of drowning babies.

"Then, son, she learned the lesson all who deal with the devil must learn sooner or later. He doesn't keep his part of the bargain. Don Antonio never loved her again, *por razón. Se murió de sentimiento por sus niños.* His last words were that he hated her and would see her in hell soon. She wasn't that lucky. She tried to undo her evil but that was impossible. The *bruja* had disappeared and none other would talk to her, much less give her any help. Priests avoided her. Church doors were slammed in her face. *La mujer se volvió loca.*"

Tony heard the words as if they were coming from God directly. His mind burned with the imagery of the story.

"She convinced herself that the children were not dead. She said they floated down the river and were waiting for her to find them and take them home. She searched all over *Tejas, Nuevo México, Arizona, California, Colorado* and *México.* She followed rivers to their end, crying for the children, but she never found them. To this day she wanders earth looking for the children, crying for them."

Tony understood. In the middle of the story he lost his fear of the woman. She was a mother looking for her lost children, a woman like his own mother who regretted giving him away and who now wanted him back. Adolfo's description of *la llorona* matched Tony's idealized vision of his mother. She was sorry. He was ready to go with her.

Tony kept his conclusions about the woman to himself. He knew no one would believe it was his mother and Jesusita would not let him go to the woods to find her. He spent hours thinking of ways to bring her to him, or to let her know where he was. He knew he could not confide in his brothers, sisters or cousins. He withdrew from them. He was quiet, subdued and surly.

The opportunity to go to the river again was provided by Johnny. The older boys treated the story of *la llorona* as a joke. They made *la llorona* faces at the young ones. They laughed at the articles in the newspaper. Johnny wanted to show everyone that *la llorona* was just another fairy story, another fantasy of old Mexicans. He decided to search the river until he found what was making the sounds and then expose it.

Johnny's idea was simple. He and his friends would go to the river around midnight, split up into pairs and search the river bank. When the sounds started the boys would converge on its source from different directions and surround whatever it was. They would have gunny sacks, knives and baseball bats. Johnny stashed one of his grandfather's rifles in the trunk of his car as a precaution.

The night of the search Johnny wore his best pair of khakis. His hair was brushed into a ducktail. A gold crucifix hung from his neck. He put a card of the Virgin Mary in his wallet. He told Jesusita he was going to a movie in Canon City and would spend the night at Paco's.

Tony decided this was his chance to be reunited with his mother. He had to keep Johnny from her. He moped around the house waiting for everyone to go to bed.

When the house was quiet he left, sneaking out the back door. He grabbed a bicycle and rode through the dark town to the river.

The heat of the day lingered on. There was a heavy, stuffy feeling in the night. Tony rode under long, dark shadows from the trees in the moonlight. The air was clean and still. Details stood out. He saw numbers on houses, hopscotch patterns on the sidewalks. Fireflies flitted around the bushes near the library where he turned onto Pikes Peak Avenue towards the river. A few bats circled the trees but he tried to ignore them. He concentrated on the woman he was going to find. He conjured up the face of his mother. She was sorrowful, loving, eager for him.

Tony parked the bicycle on the edge of the woods and walked into the darkness of the trees. He went through thick clumps of bushes and weeds on the way to the swimming hole.

The sound of the rushing water relaxed Tony. He was aware of its patterns, the consistency of its changes.

He did not see nor hear Johnny and the others. He walked along a

108 • Manuel Ramos

rocky stretch of river beach illuminated by the moon. Bright stars hung over the hills beyond the edge of the highway. A dog or coyote howled in the darkness. Owls hooted sadly.

He stared at the river, the moon, and the trees. He saw nothing. He waited and worried that she had gone. He threw flat rocks into the river, frustrated with his bad luck. He began to walk back towards the bicycle.

The crying came with a suddenness that made him jump. It started low and soft, slowly increasing in intensity. A wind stirred the trees. Their shadows danced on the ground. Tony felt as though the earth was moving. The moaning was loud, vibrant. He thought he saw shooting stars fall behind the hills. The moon passed behind a cloud and Tony was in darkness.

He heard footsteps behind him. He turned fast but there was nothing. He heard other sounds from other directions. Things seemed to move in the bushes. The moaning covered the sound of the river. The wind whipped dust around Tony in small whirlpools.

Tony realized he had made a mistake. He did not belong out there near the river looking for a woman who had drowned her children. He tried to calm himself with thoughts of his lost mother but they were not the good ones he needed. He wanted to be home with his grandmother, with the woman he loved like his own mother, with the flesh and blood person who loved him and cared for him better than any imaginary mother could. He wanted to run but he forgot where he left the bicycle. Sobs came out of his throat in hiccups.

Then he saw her. The woman in black walked towards him with her arms open. She was beautiful. Coal black eyes pierced into his, asking him to come to her. "*Hijo,* . . . *niño. Vente conmigo, tu mamá* . . . *niñooooo,* . . . *niñooooo.*" The voice was like the sound of the whistle Tony heard late at night as the train approached Florence, miles away, letting all the dogs know it was coming.

Dark red lips pursed into the kiss she blew to Tony. "*Niño,* . . . *corazón niñooooo.*" Her hands signaled for him to come to her. Tony stepped in her direction driven by a need to know his mother.

"Run, Tony, run!" Johnny hollered at his brother from a hundred yards away. Tony saw him running, holding a long stick in his hands. He started to tell Johnny it was no sweat, man, this was his mother, his old lady.

A loud hiss stopped him. His beautiful, beckoning mother had become an ugly, grotesque creature. Her skin was lumps and oozing pustules. Ragged teeth grinned evily at him. Patches of scalp gleamed beneath strands of wispy hair. The eyes were red-orange balls.

She lunged at him.

"Run, Tony, run. Get out of there!"

He felt fingernails scrape his back. He dodged her by twisting back and forth as he ran to Johnny who stood on a rise pointing the stick at the woman.

"Move you little shit. Run! Run!"

Something grabbed Tony from behind. He felt a warm slimy arm wrap around his waist. He looked into the horrible face and smelled the sweet, putrid odor he remembered from the time he found a dead chicken in the coop. He screamed. "Johnny, help! Help!" He kicked at the thing that had him. He saw a light flash, felt a thud in his back, fell to the ground and threw up. He sobbed into the earth until Johnny picked him up and carried him to the car.

Tony was in bed for a week. Old doctor Davis gave him shots of penicillin and prescribed juices but could not explain the fever, nor the long scratches on Tony's back.

He was delirious. He mumbled about his mother. He hollered for Johnny. When the fever left him he refused to talk about that night, even with Johnny.

The sounds at the river stopped. A few days after Johnny saved Tony the body of a huge bird was found on the shore of the river. The newspaper said it was a rare crane or heron that had strayed from its normal nesting place. The story speculated that the bird had been driven to the waters of the Arkansas by the unusual heat. Its long beak and spindly legs made it an object of curiosity at the firestation where it was displayed. When it decayed the firemen burned it.

Johnny tried to convince his friends that he shot *la llorona* just as she was flying off with Tony. Paco said it was no use trying to bullshit him. He was there and he had not seen anything except Tony getting sick. Paco figured Tony was out to scare his brother and his brother's friends, but had managed to scare himself instead. "Serves the little asshole right," he told Linda Garcia the night he got her drunk up on Union Mill Hill and tried to make it with her in the back of her father's Plymouth.

Adolfo knew the truth. Years later, in a place he had not known existed, he told Tony he believed him as Tony again lay in the dirt crying from fear.

"Hijo, you saw your mother for what she really was. The evil in her made her ugly. You came back home then, come with us again."

ONE STORY TOO MANY

Devon Peña

Raul had been a "good" kid until his mother died. Good like all the other kids who would visit him on those slow days when his father sent him off to his grandmother's home. If business at the store was bad, Raul usually got kicked out by his father. A scapegoat. Long-standing tradition in a family known for its obsession with tidy children. Raul was tidy. Maybe too tidy.

At his grandmother's, on those slow days before his mother's death, he would wash the coffee can full of bacon grease that his grandmother kept on the wood stove. He would wash it three times. Three times every visit. The first time to cut through the grease a bit. The second time to scrape the left-over burnt stuff from the grooves on the inside of the brim. The third time to try to get it all nice and shiny. Grandma laughed, thinking Raul was just enjoying the feel of water and soap on his perpetually dirty hands. His father, coming by to pick him up thought it all mildly disgusting and amusing. Boys shouldn't wash dishes in the kitchen. And it was even worse, Raul washed useless cans over and over again. No goals or purpose in life. Simple-minded joy from fussing over tidy, useless details.

His mother died expectedly. Always frail of body but strong in spirit, she had loved her children well enough. The husband, that was different. He was a provider. Occasionally good at it. Didn't drink and as far as she knew, he was faithful. He did, afterall, go to church with the family every Sunday and on those special days around the *posada*, Ash Wednesday, Palm Sunday, and Easter of course. Easter was special. The family would go to church and then picnic under the bridge on the road to Las Animas. That was Raul's favorite day of all the year. He would attend to his tidy details under the bridge, counting *fichas* from old soda pop bottles while the rest of the family barbequed and his mother spun out lore.

She died the third Wednesday after Raul's fifteenth bridge visit. On that visit on the Easter Sunday before her death, Raul had found something new to count under the bridge. The *huesitos* of a dead bird something or another. His sister, Celestina, had screamed at him with anger when he brought the bones over to show her. Still encrusted with a few bloody feathers, he had offered remnant wings as her share in his counting game. His mother chided Celestina.

"*Mija*, someday your very mother here will be like a dead bird with hollowed eyes and broken wings." She counted the left wing bones with Raul. There were 36 bones. A good number, Raul reassured her.

"You will live 36 years more, *mamita*. I'll be grown up by then and can take care of you from Daddy." The father, naturally, had scowled.

Two months after the death, the father remarried. She was a long-standing lover of his. They had met seventeen years earlier. Celestina had just been born. It had been a difficult pregnancy and the father quickly got frustrated. The C-section turned him off and he constantly complained about the lack of sex with his wife.

"Luisita, the Church says you have to give me as many children as I want. We need many. It will make me a strong family. Besides, I need . . . I would really like a son, someone to help with the store when I start to get older."

She was already ill. The pregnancy had filled her up like a hot balloon she always thought. Now, she felt like she was torn up inside. She was getting too old to have as many kids as he wanted. She refused

114 • Devon Peña

him. It was her right she thought to herself. And besides, somewhere out there God must agree that an ill woman should not be an open womb for her husband's desires. Raul's conception had been even more difficult. He had wanted her pregnant before her healing was complete. She made him wait a year before she would even let him enter her again. In the meantime, he had gone about his selfish affair.

Stepmother Grace was younger. She was thin, dark-haired, and had wispy green eyes. She liked dressing up for her new husband. Raul's father craved her and got plenty from her. She and Raul did not get along well. She despised his looks, too much like that bitch mother of his she thought. Kept me apart from my man for 15 years.

Three weeks after Grace moved in, Raul's father forced him out of the house.

"*Cabrón, hijo de perra*! You were never worth anything. Get the fuck out of my home! Go count your fingers on the street corner!" He screamed incessantly for an hour at Raul. Raul's travesty? He had accidentally dropped a box of wedding china, a gift to the newlyweds from Grace's great aunt. Slipped on a damn piece of *plátano*.

Raul resisted. "*Papá*, you can't just throw me out. Will you?"

His father battered him with a wrench. Cracked his skull. A clean wedge of steel slicing through Raul's bushy thick black hair. Celestina, afraid of similar treatment, dragged the boy out the door, into her half-running Chevy Impala. Dropped him off in the parking lot of Las Animas General Hospital, and drove off. She never saw the family again.

Raul was in the hospital for two weeks. Social welfare workers got wind of the incident and terminated parental rights. As far as Grace and her husband were concerned, they were welcome to it. Raul was placed with temporary foster parents, bouncing from one wretched experience to another. Finally, on the first Wednesday after his eighteenth birthday he became a runaway. Running from anguish, from pain, from the constant battering by faceless, nameless guardians.

Raul ended-up in Denver. Five-points; under the bridge; hideaway. It was November, 1983 and a colder than usual winter. He quickly learned the rules of urban survival. His new and only friend, an old *gabacho* transient from the rural Ohio River Valley, taught him survival. How to wrap himself up in newspaper to keep warm in the freezing snow and ice. To hang around laundromats in the early evening, keeping warm next to the clothes dryers, scavanging the garbage cans in the alley for the night's meal. Staying off Colfax to avoid the street patrols. Owning nothing but the clothes on his back, the shoes on his feet, and an old tattered plastic bag to carry stuff in. More bridge life was in waiting for Raul.

"Never know when one has to get up and move fast," the *gabacho* would explain, "best be ready by having everything you need on you."

Raul's new friend even enjoyed counting games. And in his new urban home Raul found countless things to count. His favorite counting game was to sit at the laundromat and count the number of tumbles a specific shirt or dress or pants took in a dryer. He could count until the thousands before the *gabacho* pulled him away for the evening's meal hunt.

The first Monday morning in December came and went. Ten inches of snow covered the asphalt expanses of his new home. That night, on his walk to the laundromat, he was assaulted. Mugged by some young, teenish punks. Took his thrift shop wool coat and his black shoes. Barefoot and barebacked he staggered back to his bridge refuge. No newspapers, only his three cubic foot carton box where he slept, his pants, a t-shirt, and his own sinewy brown skin for warmth. Raul's toes froze. His *gabacho* friend found him, called the EMS, and went with him to the hospital. Raul was delirious and confused.

The doctors struggled to get him to let them even touch him. He could not feel a thing in his toes and was numbed out, raw nerve endings seething from the tips of his come-back-to-life fingers to his swollen, bruised eyes. He kept looking at the floor tiles of the emergency room.

"*Mamita*. I count for you now, I count . . . the days, the nights, they count, I count because they are there . . . the *cuadros*, they are there . . . here? Where? (Cowering in the corner, with fear gripping him, glancing sideways at the doctors). Its OK *mamita*, I know you hungry for it too. It go away soon . . . it go come away with me and everyone else too, they count with us, *mamita*, they hold my fingers apart, want to kill me, hurt me . . . me not hurt noone . . . me hurt you, hurt Daddy, hurt Cesi."

Whispering to his colleague, the doctor observed:

"Seems schizophrenic to me, Dan."

"Yes, ahem. I'd say this constitutes a basis to get this kid on meds. What do you think? Prolixin?"

"Yea, that should do very nicely. Get him down a bit so we can

116 • Devon Peña

work on his toes. We'll never get those suckers off unless we zap him out a bit."

"Well, OK. No identification?"

"No. Only thing he had was something that looked like some bird bones in his pant pockets."

"Well . . . you better make sure Nurse Wilson gets a psychosocial history and functioning level blurp on him before we release him. Never know, those audits for the Medicaid are an awful bother. Just make sure its all down on paper."

"What about follow-up?"

"Ah . . . ahem . . . well, let's see. Get him some Thorazine. A good 90 days supply. No need to have him coming around here too soon again. Oh, yes. Make it a very strong dosage."

DIAMOND EYES AND PIG TAILS

Alfredo de la Torre

They are closing the steel bars behind me. Now they close with electrical computers, and as I'm walking with the guard on my side, I realize we are going downwards thru corridors with cold walls. I'm not yet accustomed to my new prisoner's uniform, and for the first time I'm afraid that I may not survive in this prison. I know from the last of my buddies, who came out of this prison, that there are three violent gangs: The Sindicate of la Raza, the Africans of the blacks, and the Nazis of the gringos. The gangs are at war, and they kill each other very often. The situation is out of control, and the politicians have known for years that there are too many prisoners in this jail. The violence was started by the guards with torture, and with their pigs (prisoners who help the guards) willing to beat up and assassinate. The politicians have promised a future prison. Now we are going down by elevator on this last building that has been constructed, but I also know there are many other prisoners, at other units, who live in tents. I start to get a phobia just thinking that the only light I would get to see would be electric. Is it possible that the judge really gave me a life sentence? I'm a political prisoner in the United States; for daring to speak against the government and for organizing Prison Reforms.

Now in my cell, reclined on my cot at the top, I keep thinking. The three kids were drinking beer in the car that was parked in the dark outside the store. I just went to buy milk when all of a sudden they yelled at me from the car. —You old fucker!— I was the only one passing by, but I ignored them. I went in the store all pissed off, bought the milk, and when I came out I heard the same voice coming from the car. —Come here, you old bastard!— This time I saw the teenager very well. With his purple shirt and a beer on his hand, he moved away from the car to where I was walking and he got in my way, so I stopped. The other two never came out of the car. I was ready to cross him with a right, when teenager number four comes out of nowhere with a gun pointing at my head. I saw him determined to shoot, and quickly I dropped the milk and grabbed for the gun, but I felt the first shot entering thru one side of my forehead and out thru one side of my ear. I was still able to grab his hand and we struggled for the gun while I was losing blood in spurts. Then another shot hit me on a leg and after that I was able to take the gun away from him. I shot him once in the stomach and I fainted. When I woke up, I was already in the hospital with a policeman on the door. What a chance that the other guy died of two shots, and the gun turned out to be, my gun, and the three witnesses against me, and I against a racist judge, and all the fury of the beast unleashed against me. I heard the laugh of the guard pig, and after the laugh the threat. —I'm going to let you out to do some play time with the others, but no conversations about politics or prison reforms.— I had already decided to do a silent time with the hope of getting out of here some day.

I went out to the playground patio, and I picked a place where I sat with my back to the wall. The pigs were strolling and moving their tails to scare the flies away. At the height of the walls; the superior guards, with diamond eyes and their machine guns, were watching us. The prisoners were very involved in their activities and their conversations; and a terror, that my assassin is amongst them, possessed me. Two Chicano brothers who look like twins start arguing with loud voices as if they are going to fight. I realize that close to them sits a Don

120 • Alfredo de la Torre

Chicano, advanced in age, and he is surrounded by others who seem to respect him. The twins continue with their argument trying to impress Don Chicano, who now laughs. It's all about trying to prove who is more macho. One twin pushes the other one, who falls and does a pantomime on the floor followed by a few flips in the air, and everybody laughs. Then the two twins charge towards me, and they make an attempt to scare me. Other chicanos also surround me and I can't breathe well. I stand up and I go to Don Chicano as he looks at me with a smile. He is playing cards with others, and I stand by his side to look at his cards. He stops smiling and he makes a play with a card. Everything is silence. Three pigs are watching the game without moving their tails. All the rest of the prisoners also come near. I snap that Don Chicano is playing against a gay, a Nazi, and an African. The gay with grey hair drops his cards and gives up. He gets up while the others keep playing, and he stands besides me, taking my hand. Don Chicano talks with a deep voice to the gay, while he plays another card of great importance.

—Leave him alone Roque.

The gay lets my hand loose, and he dedicates himself to watch the game with great attention. After a while the Nazi and the African declare themselves losers, and Don Chicano stands up to give the good news to everybody.

—All the gang wars are suspended until after the big dance of Güero Polkas.

Everybody screams full of happiness; the twins flip several times, caps of prisoners fly up on the air, the pigs move their tails; and the electric lights go off. The diamond eyes turn on and off, and a punk rock music appears to be the signal for the gays to kiss on the mouth. A frightening disorder takes place and I see my assassin getting close to me with a dagger, but I get lost in the dark. I run with my hands to the wall. A secret door opens and I wind up in a narrow corridor. I run not knowing where I'm going, making turns and going up and down like a crossword puzzle.

It's a rainy morning and Don Chicano and I sit on a bench inside a baseball player's hut. We are waiting for the rain to stop and the soft drops make us sleepy. In front of us are the tennis courts that we have to sweep where they have the small holes. Behind the tennis courts are the homes of the guards. The houses are hidden behind green trees and further back, up high amongst the clouds the sun already starts to give his light. It's a beautiful scene and I'm no longer afraid of anything. We continue to wait in silence until we see two tall men who get ready to play in one of the courts. I want to tell them to wait until we sweep the water holes, but they are already hitting the ball that flies thru the air in slow motion. I realize the court where they play is as big as a football field. The game is suspended and quickly we sweep the holes. The giants with diamond eyes thank us, and we go to another court.

We are already working more relaxed. We organize territory like furrows in the cotton fields, and we move on thru an imaginary line that permits us to be close to one another and we are able to talk. We keep going until we reach the net and then we return thru another imaginary line. We talk about the brutal work being done by other prisoners in the cotton fields, and I thank Don Chicano for getting me this job. He reminds me about the Aztlan Cultural Committee, and he shows me two tickets to a sacrifice. The death execution of a prisoner promises to be a great show. He invites me and I understand that his friendship is honest, but I tell him that the death penalty should not exist in this country. He turns furious and tells me that the prisoner they are about to execute is a sex maniac who has raped and killed many women. I tell him Sodom U.S.A. is the guilty. He asks me to be more clear and I deal the cards more slowly.

—First Point: The sex maniac—a mentally ill person who commits a crime. Second Point: The judges—representatives of the government and the laws. This government permits women to get naked so money can be made of her. Pornography; books, movies, commercials, television, and on the street they let women walk around almost naked. In this government, sin is called freedom. Sex, sex, everywhere they show it to you. What if the person already has a weak mind? Third Point: Justice—one for another. If we are going to kill one from the first point, let's kill one from the second point also. You all didn't like that, did you? The least they could do is lock up for life those from the first point, and don't ever let them out again. In a country where there is no justice, there should not be a death penalty. And now even men come out on television with their tiny panties and their ballies hanging . . .

—Enough, stop!

Don Chicano gets angry. —You shouldn't be talking about politics. I read your novel where you talk about that. — I argue that I can repeat myself as much as I want to, and he calmly pulls down his trousers and shows me his behind. I see that from a small hole on his underdrawers comes out a tiny pig tail undergoing development. In all fours, he speaks to me fully decided.

— Pull it off!

With joy I grab the tail and pull with both hands but it's very hard. Finally I pull out the small tail with the entire root, and I throw it towards the grass on one side of the court. He puts on his trousers and wipes off the sweat of his forehead with the sleeve of his shirt. Very calm he shows me the two tickets for the prisoner's execution. He tears one up, throws it towards the grass and says proudly.

— The one I tore up is mine, but I'm going to sell this other one. He charges at me with his philosophy on the need to survive, and he confesses to me that he makes deals with everybody except those who fuck gays. He says this very serious, and I tell him that he doesn't have to worry about me. The sun is already out in full force, and we continue working hard with the brooms. We change to another court, looking for holes where the water accumulates. In reality they are not holes, but rather parts of the court where the level was not accomplished to perfection. By now the giants are hitting the ball so hard that the sound echos all over the sky. For a while I'm marveled watching them play. Don Chicano interrupts me and tells me about his participation in the cultural events, and his relationship with the Mayor Guard of the prison. It's important that the violence between the prisoners diminish, and the possibility exists that once again they would let us be separate from the Africans and the Nazis. The dance of Güero Polkas would be only for Chicanos. He tells me that the Mayor Guard recognizes my work in Prison Reforms, and he wants us to work together, but no politics; just cultural events, dances, mariachis, Indian dancers, and other witchcraft. If I cooperate, my life would be respected. I accept.

I listen calmly to the classical music as I look up. I'm laying on top of several bags of white cloth. These are bulks of normal size tied with white strings. I also wear a white uniform. I'm inside an enormous room and the walls are very high with no visible doors. I have been locked up for a long time in this subterranean hole.

I remember my job so I start moving the bags from one side of the room to the other side. I feel lonely and sad with this job, and I see that thousands of bags still need to be moved. Located in the center of the room are some steel machines that I don't recognize. I keep working for several hours, and as my work advances, more steel machines are exposed. I suddenly stop as I hear a noise, and I jump to hide among the bags. The noise comes from behind the machines. It's the Nazi and the African who are dressed in white the same as I. It seems they were asleep on the machines. They are now oiling the machines. Both of them talk in seriousness about the job that needs to be done in this room. After a while, they proudly begin to move the bags with the machines.

I come out of my hiding place, and I go to work as the classical music continues without stopping. Tonight is the dance of Güero Polkas, and I'm terrorized to think how I'm going to get out of here. The African guesses my thoughts and stops working with his machine. He is a tall and slim black of about fifty, and he has a noble glance. He tells me he is the boss in this laundry, and he orders me to undress. I obey, and with one of his machines he gives me a steam bath, followed by a shower with cold water. I dry myself with a white towel as the Nazi opens one of the bags with clean clothes, and he gives me the underdrawers, the undershirt, and the socks. Then he surprises me when from a clothes hanger covered with plastic, he takes out my brown trousers for going out, and the blue shirt I had left in the free world. The African gives me my tangerine shoes and the hair oil and a mirror. I don't need to shave. How strange that my beard has never grown in this jail.

"Now comes the good part," says the African in English. "We have enough electricity to get this thing up only once." He pulls a few handles on a machine, and he makes me climb on a small platform where I can't grab a hold from anywhere, and I have to remain standing. The platform goes up high. It keeps stretching like a long arm from the machine, and when it stretches as far as it reaches, it's going to return downward. It jerks strongly several times and I almost fall. The machine reaches up until I'm close to a steel door that's closed. I have to jump when the machine stops and I'm frozen with fright. I feel the machine starting to move to return downward, and then I jump. I'm standing with my belly and my hands almost stuck to the steel door. My shoes' heels are hanging on the air and I'm losing my balance. I think about the laundry bags, and maybe the fall wouldn't be fatal. I must not look down, I must not think like that. I push the door and it doesn't open. I position my feet in such a way that I'm now standing firm. An enormous faith grabs a hold of me. I close my eyes for a while, and when I open them again, before me I encounter the complete scene of a night club.

The mood is set at half light; there is smoke, tables, men and women, and a dance floor in the center. Everybody is wearing civilian clothes, but I recognize they are all jail birds. Some men who are standing close to me are looking towards the edge of the dance floor where several women sit by themselves, and they comment that all the women are also prisoners. I walk forward and I see only raza people. In front of me, a small table is occupied by two men. On my left side sits Don Chicano, in front of me an empty chair, and on the right side sits the gay, Roque. Both of them appear to be talking seriously and making a deal. After a while Don Chicano points for me to sit, and I sit on the center chair. Suddenly the lights go off and out comes Güero Polkas yelling, — Free, Free! — The hand claps and the screams of happiness began to quiet down as the Aztec dancers enter with the incense, and everybody quietly observes. The announcer, who looks a bit like Borrao Enamorao, introduces himself as the responsible one for bringing the dancers, and thru the microphone he explains the symbolism of the ceremony.

Then the drums followed by the dances, and the color feathers flying thru the air. Don Chicano somewhat displeased tells us that the Mayas were the superior tribe, but Roque makes the point that even so, the Aztecs were the last great civilization in power, and they borrowed from the Mayas the same as the Romans took from the Greeks to build their empire. They want to get me involved in their argument, but I don't let them and I tell them that I'm a man of this time. The last dance of the serpent is executed, and winding thru a door the dancers leave. Everyone applauds except me. Don Chicano elbows me and tells me to applaud. I tell him I don't believe in priests, rites or ceremonies. He tells me not to be such a rebel, and that anyway I should applaud for the diamond eyes. I remember I'm part of the Aztlan Cultural Committee-Prison Reforms-Stop the Violence. I applaud against my will and drink from a glass containing orange juice. Everyone is drinking non-alcoholic beverages, and I notice all the waiters are Nazis and Africans. Don Chicano tells me that when they have their events, we are going to be the waiters. Then Borrao Enamorao comes close to me from my left side. My childhood friend. The one who would take away our girlfriends, the one who owes me money, the con of all cons, the one who knows all the tricks and the ones he doesn't know he will invent. More than twenty years without seeing him, and now look where this crazy fool appears. With his winning smile, very gentle, he speaks to me softly. —I am an attorney and I am working on the free world with some other lawyers. I came because I was told you were here. We are finding new evidence in your case, and there is hope to get you out of here. — Then he stands up straight and with his cat eyes, he sees how Roque is melting and smiling at him. Don Chicano looks at them with disgust. I become embarrassed with the situation. I don't like what's happening. I need the help of Don Chicano. The music begins to play. Still sitting down, Roque speaks to Borrao. —Shall we dance?— Borrao answers with pleasure. —Let's go.— Roque stands up, and they both face each other on the dance floor in front of us. Then suddenly Borrao says to Roque. —I'll take the one in the green dress and you take the other one.— Borrao takes off to dance with the one in the green dress and Roque stands still. What a relief I feel. Both of us very happy, Don Chicano and I, get up and two gals agree to dance with us. I mix amongst the crowd and the dance floor gets full of people. The dark one I'm dancing with has long black hair, and she wears a black silk dress. Borrao is already up in front of the dance floor singing with his guitar like Pelvis.

High above us I see the guards with their machine guns. The lights go off. The guards start to shine thru their diamond eyes. I'm able to penetrate the strong light, and behind the machine guns sits the Mayor Guard on a big chair. He is accompanied by the politicians, the Indians with their feathers, and some religious leaders. Once again an enormous faith grabs a hold of me. You will get me out of this hell Borrao. The gays and the lesbians are already dancing on the dance floor and they kiss on the mouth. I keep dancing with the dark one, and she lets me caress her long hair. I lower my hand and down there where I told you about, hidden with her hair, I feel a small tail undergoing development. She breathes hard as I kiss her, and holding the tail tight with my hand, I whisper softly in her ear.

—Can I pull it off?

126 • Alfredo de la Torre

A DOLLAR'S WORTH

O.J. Valdez

"But I told you I have no money, Don Martín." The slight old man, squinting through old-fashioned rimless glasses, seemed to grow smaller, as though the words had taken too much of his substance with them. His unkempt appearance was emphasized all the more by the grizzled growth of whiskers on his chin. He took a thick bundle of folded-up newspapers tied with string from under his arm and laid it on the counter. Then, reaching under his frayed, black woolen overcoat layered with an even coating of whitish dust he pulled out a worn leather coin purse. He opened it and emptied it on the counter next to the newspapers.

"See," he said, sliding the coins toward the storekeeper with his hand, "only twenty-three cents. And I've got to have something to eat for Tisne and myself."

Across the counter of the small neighborhood grocery deep in the Westside of San Antonio the owner, Perfecto Martín, a short, fat man with a fringe of black hair surrounding his bald, smoothly round head, slowly lowered his bulk onto a wooden stool with a grunt. He looked at the coins disinterestedly.

"Look, Goyo, it's nothing to me. You owe me thirty-seven dollars and eighty-five cents," he said, pointing to a worn blue school composition book which lay open on the counter. "Until that's paid in full, you'll get no more credit from me."

The storekeeper reached into his shirt pocket and drew out a single cigarette. From under the counter he pulled out a box of kitchen matches, one of which he struck with his thumbnail. He raised the sputtering flame to his cigarette. Exhaling blue smoke from his nostrils, he leaned back on the stool.

Goyo looked at the cigarette hungrily. He ran his tongue over his lips once, and then again. In a voice that quavered, he said, "All I need is a loaf of bread and a little bit of *chorizo*, and maybe a bone or two for Tisne. At most a dollar's worth. And I know I'll have some money Monday — I was promised some yard work out on Ruiz Street. Forty-three years I've been doing jobs for people *en el barrio* that they don't want to do themselves. Whatever I make Monday I'll bring to you, every penny, to put on my bill — I swear it."

Perfecto, the cigarette dangling from a corner of his mouth, stared at Goyo with narrowed eyes. "You've got to understand my position," he said. "I can't operate on credit. I've got bills to pay too, you know." He paused. In the silence, above the hissing of the gas heater in the corner, the moaning wind of a late February norther slowly rose and fell, rattling the heavy wooden doors of the store in an alternating rhythm.

"It's not that I don't trust you; I've got to draw the line somewhere." He pulled out the package of cigarettes and, as if to lend weight to his argument, offered it to the old man, who reached for it with fingers that trembled noticeably.

Goyo took one, hesitated and then, with a questioning look to Don Martín, who nodded, took another and gave back the pack as he pocketed both cigarettes. "*Muchas gracias,*" he said.

For a long time he stared at the loaded trays of steaks, roasts and cold cuts in the glass front refrigerator case to the right of the counter. Finally he sighed. "Very well. Let me have twenty cents' worth of neck bones — for Tisne," he said emphatically.

Martín got up and walked slowly to the meat case. He seemed

deep in thought as he wrapped several large, almost bare bones, the small slivers of meat nearly invisible on them. Suddenly the wind blew open the front door, sending a blast of icy air through the store. Don Martín stumbled awkwardly around the counter and slammed the doors shut. As he walked back to the meat case the puzzled expression on his face had vanished, replaced by one of purposeful vision. He took two links of sausage from the case and wrapped these, placing them on the counter with the bones. Then he walked over to the bread rack and got two small loaves of bread, and with some coffee and sugar from a nearby shelf, dropped everything in a brown paper bag.

"But—but I cannot pay," Goyo said.

"Don't worry; this is all going on your account," the grocer said. He took three eggs from a wire basket on the counter and put them in the bag, too. "For breakfast tomorrow," he said.

"*Muchísimas gracias*, Don Martín," Goyo said as he picked up the newspapers and the bag of groceries. "May God repay your generosity."

"I'm beginning to think that's the only way your bill will ever be paid," Don Martín said with a scowl. "Go on, be off. But remember, no more credit after this."

Smiling, the old man stopped on his way to the door and looked back. "I'll be back Monday with some money, you'll see."

Outside, a shaggy black dog with a single white patch on its muzzle jumped up, its tail wagging furiously, and circled back and forth in front of Goyo as he limped along in the pale, lemon-colored evening light. Goyo huddled down inside the threadbare overcoat as the sharp wind buffeted him with heavy gusts. After a short walk around the corner, he continued down a narrow alley lined with cramped little houses standing elbow to elbow. He turned at a dilapidated wooden gate just before a striped black and white wooden barricade in the middle of the alley. Alazan Creek was just beyond the barricade. He walked across the small yard of bare, hard-packed dirt. With a key tied to a string on his belt, he unlocked the heavy padlock on the front door of a small weatherbeaten shack. The dog ran inside eagerly.

"You're hungry, eh, Tisne." The old man put his bundles down on a small wooden table and closed the door. He slid home the two bolts, one at the top and one at the bottom of the door, and placed a heavy two-by-four on two brackets across the middle.

"Just let me get a fire going and then we can eat," he said as he removed his coat and folded it carefully over the back of the single chair.

A DOLLAR'S WORTH • 129

The only other piece of furniture was an old rusty cot, unmade, with a heavy army surplus blanket rumpled up in a pile on top. It took up most of one wall. A heavy iron stove stood in the middle of the room.

Goyo untied the bundle of newspapers and started rolling them up into small, thick logs, tying them with string. He opened the stove and arranged several of these inside. The rest he piled carefully on the floor beside it. Soon a blazing fire was cheering up the drab room.

"That's much better, isn't it?" He directed his question to the dog. He set the eggs carefully in a small bowl on the window sill. The glass in the single frame had long since been replaced by cardboard. The bread and sausage he arranged carefully on the table. "Ah, I almost forgot," he said as he rubbed his hands together briskly. "You should remind me of these things, Tisne." The dog, lying by the warm stove, wagged his tail.

The old man picked up the black overcoat from the chair and spread it out on the bed. Lifting a corner of the worn lining, he removed a small oblong package wrapped in a piece of grease-stained cloth which was pinned to the coat underneath. Glancing at the window, he said, "If the wrong people saw us it would go real bad for us, Tisne. No one must ever find out our little secret." He folded back the rag. Inside was a small stack of one dollar bills. "This is the time of day I enjoy most," he said, "when we put away our day's wages."

He reached under the table and pulled out a rusty gallon can. After pouring a little water from a bucket into it, he stirred the contents carefully. Satisfied, he dabbed a small dot of the paste on a dollar bill from the stack on the table. He stuck it on the newspaper covering the wall. Then another, and another. "We must prepare for old age, Tisne," he said. "No one will look after us when I can no longer work." He stuck three, five, ten, twenty-three one-dollar bills on the wall; all the contents of the package. Finally he covered them with three sheets of newspaper, sticking one over the other carefully.

"There," he said, wiping his hands. He surveyed the room. All four walls were completely covered with newspaper, in some places so thick that they looked like the padded walls of a cell in some asylum. "We should have enough to retire on soon, Tisne. Maybe in another year or two." Unwrapping the sausage, he said, "Come, let's eat supper now."

THE WEIGHT LIFTERS

David Nava Monreal

The three of them: Hector, Pete and Henry, dawdled in the backyard all summer lifting weights. Hector was the skinny one, a hundred and ten pounds soaking wet, his hair was a bristly patch and his front tooth was chipped from falling off his bike while coasting down Rocky Hill without brakes. Pete was more muscular, thick-necked, he had a weak left eye that flashed whitely in the sunlight; he didn't talk much but he grunted pig-like as he tried to bench press two hundred and ten pounds. Henry was the handsome one of the trio—lighthaired, hazel-eyes—he was also the firebrand intellectual who at the age of fifteen had read Voltaire, Theodore Dreiser and a smattering of Albert Camus. He regularly spouted adages and drank too much and whenever there was a session of "pumping iron" he would "kill" three Buds while impressing his gullible friends with great feats of strength.

A week ago he lifted one hundred and seventy pounds over his head, held it for ten seconds, then flung the barbells down with a clatter.

"Man, you can really lift," Hector sighed while wiping beads of sweat off his forehead.

"It's all mental. Prepare yourself and think nothing but positive thoughts."

Pete lumbered over, his thick glasses dangling from his glossy nose. He was wearing a tattered sweat-shirt and a black pair of high-top tennis shoes.

"Shit, I can do better than that."

Henry was cool, his poise was only surpassed by his handsomeness. "Bullshit."

"I can prove it."

Hector was often anxious for his competing friends, they usually tried to out do each other then ended up pulling muscles.

"Be careful, Pete, the last time you almost got a hernia."

"Ah, step aside."

Pete bent down, gripped the barbell; he prepared himself. He puffed up his cheeks, took a deep breath, squatted down, closed his eyes then opened the weak one while waiting for the right moment. One second passed, then two, with a huge groan and veins bulging from his neck, he lifted. The bar reached his chest, chains of spittle flew out of his mouth, with a mammoth effort he tried putting the weight above his head. Nothing doing; he rocked precariously, then he dropped the weights, nearly stubbing his toe.

Henry laughed, flashing his perfect teeth, "I told you you couldn't do it."

Pete stared at his friends, his weak eye looked there and everywhere, "Well, I got all summer, wait and see, Mr. Schwarzenegger."

It was the highlight of their lives lifting weights in Hector's backyard. They were all seventeen years old and what they had in common was their need to be men. They were also the oddities of the Mexican *barrio*. None of them belonged to gangs nor did they steal cars nor did they have any plans of dropping out of high school in the near future. An attitude like that was dangerous in a rough neighborhood like Boyle Heights. Most of the other boys their ages were defiant rough-necks, most of them slept with a sawed-off shotgun stuffed under their beds and none of them were clamoring to get into Notre-Dame. And Hector

132 • David N. Monreal

was the first boy to ever say he wanted to be a doctor, then Pete followed suit by saying he wanted to be a businessman, then, of course, the soigne Henry announced that he was going to be the first Chicano Norman Mailer.

"Who in the hell is Norman Mailer?" Hector asked one day as all three of them walked down the street together.

"A writer."

"I never heard of him."

"That's because you never read, dumb-shit."

"I read medical journals."

"All the wrong stuff."

Pete twisted his eyes around in order to look through his thick glasses, "What did this Norman Mailer write, Mr. Einstein?"

"At the age of twenty-six he wrote the greatest novel ever written. It was called THE NAKED AND THE DEAD."

Pete squinted in the sunlight, "Shit, the bum wrote dirty books."

"Don't be stupid." Henry replied.

"They had to be dirty books. What's this crap about naked and dead people?"

Henry liked edifying his ignorant admirers, "You guys are never going to make it out of this neighborhood if you keep being as dumb as you are. You've got to expand beyond Pico Rivera and El Monte. Maybe if you spend more time in the library you'd be able to keep up with me . . . Norman Mailer wrote the most vivid prose around, you could smell the decaying jungles . . ."

Hector interrupted the sage with a rickety, insecure voice, "If I spend any more time at the library I could get myself killed."

"What do you mean?" Henry asked.

"Chango and his gang were waiting outside for me last night. They shoved me around and threw my books on the sidewalk. They told me if they seen me coming out of the library again they were going to hang my balls out to dry."

"Those sonofabitches," snapped Pete.

"Why didn't you tell us earlier?" Henry said.

"I didn't think it was important."

"It's the most important event in our young lives. We have to take a philosophical stance against those thugs." Henry excitedly explained, "We have to show them that we can't be pushed around. I won't stand for it."

"But what can we do?" Asked Hector.

"A lot."

"Yeah," Pete added, "that's why we're lifting weights in the first place."

"That's one of the reasons," Henry said, "But we also lift weights to give us the sense of courage and wisdom. When a man is powerful and confident he can tell the world the perfect truth. It's more than just building muscles, it's building lucidity."

Hector smiled even though some of Henry's metaphysics went over his head, but he was happy that his co-horts were willing to back him up. "You guys are great, the best friends I ever had. Come on, let's go down to my backyard, my mother will fix us a pitcher of iced tea while we pump iron."

A month passed and still there was a mess of huffing and puffing in the backyard. Hector hadn't gained a pound. There were small lumps growing on both his arms just below the elbows and he loved flexing them in front of the full length mirror leaning against the wooden fence. Pete was the one making the most dramatic progress. His biceps had enlarged by several inches and his chest nearly burst out of his faded sweatshirt. But, of course, he was the hardest worker, he took weight lifting seriously, there was only one thing on his mind, to beat Henry, no matter how much pain was involved. Then Henry, as expected, didn't do much but depend on his natural abilities. Once in a while he worked-out but only marginally; most of the time he sipped on Millers — sometimes Coors — and criticized the techniques being used by his buddies. According to him, Hector was using too much arm and Pete, well, his upper torso would have the dimensions of a rhinoceros if he didn't start working out his legs. Anyway, weight lifting was a matter of intelligence and wisdom and not just of brute strength.

It was all fun, but when they weren't lifting weights they were out in the streets of Los Angeles, looking for girls or just wasting time between studying and reading. Olvera Street was a favorite hang-out. There the girls were citified and glittery, most of them spoke perfect English, and it was rumored that they would do anything for trinkets and a ride in a BMW. One night Henry came across a living doll. She had beautiful black hair, gleaming dark eyes and a birthmark next to her tiny mouth. Her name was Esther Gomez; Henry bought her a Coke and a *pan dulce* while her two younger girlfriends giggled in the background.

134 • David N. Monreal

"I got a lot of money." Henry lied.

"Oh yeah?"

"Yeah, I write for magazines. Stories, articles, things like that."

"What magazines do you write for?"

"Cosmopolitan, New Yorker, you know, the best."

"I read Cosmopolitan and I never seen your stuff in there."

"I write under a pen name. Change it every week."

By that time Hector and Pete were musculing in, trying to share in some of the action.

"Hey, why don't you introduce us?" Pete said.

"Nah, I ain't got time."

"Why not, Mr. Writer?"

Esther blushed, her long lashes batted like Chinese fans, "You're a writer for real!"

"Of course I am."

Esther waved her friends over. They were between thirteen and sixteen years old; both were pretty and both were wearing tight Jordache jeans.

"Meet a real true to life writer."

"A writer?" The younger one blurted.

Henry smiled dashingly then pulled at an invisible carvat, "Let me introduce you to my colleagues. Hector Garcia, Pete Alvarez meet . . ."

They ran into the night giggling and laughing. They found a summer movie and sat up in the balcony. Half-way through the car chase scene, Henry took beautiful Esther into the darkest corner and kissed her while telling her that she was inspiration, his muse. She only smiled and tried her best to keep her virtue.

At eleven o'clock all six of them poured out of the show, flushed red and a little disheveled. They walked through the blazing storm of flashing neons and speeding cars; Mexican music lifted into the warm night and each of them individually believed that they had fallen in love. After walking the girls home, the boys stopped off at an open air coffee shop and sipped on Cokes. Like usual, Henry lied, he said he had conquered sweet Esther without being caught in his act of passion. Hector and Pete didn't know whether to believe him or not, he spun such a good tale.

Around midnight they scattered into the streets; Hector split off and disappeared around a corner. It had been a heady evening, they had met lovely girls and that was plenty of stuff to dream on.

The next morning Pete and Henry knocked on Hector's door. Minutes later, Hector's mother stood at the threshold, her hair drooping over her face.

"What did you boys do last night?" She screamed.

"Nothing."

"My poor Hector is in the hospital. Tell me what happened!"

A half-hour later, Pete and Henry were sitting around Hector's bed. A fat nurse with tinted hair was wiping his brow. His eyes were swollen and the color of eggplant. The doctor stepped in and told the boys that Hector had taken a serious beating, he had two broken ribs and maybe a fractured skull. It wasn't until Tuesday — three days later — that Hector was able to talk.

"What the hell happened?" Pete asked.

"They jumped me in the dark." Hector's lips were bruised so he talked out of the right corner of his mouth, "Chango and his crew. They came out of nowhere. Chango hit me when I wasn't looking."

Henry was riled, his hands even shook, "Why?"

"They said I was fooling around with the wrong girl. They said that the girl belonged to their *barrio* . . ." Hector was nearly crying, he hurt all over, "They said I was trespassing on their territory."

"Bastards!" Pete said.

"We got to do something about it," Henry hissed, "we got to get even."

It took Hector about two and a half weeks to get into reasonable shape. He spent most of that time at home in the backyard, sitting under the shady fig tree, drinking iced-tea while Henry and Pete worked at the weights more vigorously than ever. Henry especially had become a man possessed. He didn't drink anymore nor fool around; he had bought a book on weight lifting and he followed every chapter religiously. From eight o'clock in the morning until noon, Henry and Pete did their exercises while Hector rooted them on. They even drank vitamins; it wasn't long before some results began to show.

Pete became more bulky, almost muscle-bound. His normally large neck had grown twice its size and his pectorals and biceps were inflated like water balloons. Henry developed in an entirely different way. He became sleek, hard, his slender body became a graceful topography of muscles; there wasn't an ounce of fat on him and he even began to move with more buoyancy than before. Both boys worked on the weights silently, it had become apparent that they had a mission to accomplish and nothing was going to deter them from their goal.

For many hours they grunted and groaned, sweat poured down their faces, all the while Hector drank tea and watched them with amazement. He had never seen Henry work so hard; he had always thought that Henry was a bit lazy, more than that, a lot lazy, but for the past several weeks Henry had gone through a transformation. Not only did he lift weights, he adopted them. They became part of his personality, every time he lifted them it was as though he was meditating or going into a trance. He often spoke about the wisdom and truth one obtained from strength, but that was philosophy, Hector was only impressed by Henry's dedication.

By the middle of the third week Henry brought in a whole new element into their training; he had gone down to the library and checked out a book on karate. It was a huge book illustrated with action pictures and stances. The boys — even Hector — stood around the backyard simulating kicks and swings. They had read the book together and now they were trying to practice what they had learned.

Henry was the leader, he showed the boys what was proper and what was not, "You see, it's all in the movements, in body control." He would demonstrate by slowly spinning his body around, his right leg dangling in mid-air, "Make believe that you're a bird or any kind of graceful animal. Karate is taken from nature. The Chinese discovered that all animals have an instinctive inner defense. That's because they understand themselves . . ."

Hector stood up, some gauzy bandages were still wrapped around his ribs. He spun around, shakily, his feet got tangled in the grass, and with a thud he fell down to the ground. He moaned a little as his mother's red face popped out of the kitchen window. "What's going on out there?"

"Nothing, mother." Hector groaned.

"Are you *loco* or something?"

"No, we're just practicing karate, Mrs. Garcia," Henry explained, "It's nothing to worry about."

"You look like a bunch of nuts." She yelled, "Just be careful."

Hector dragged himself off the ground and wheezed, "It ain't gonna work, man, it's useless."

"What do you mean?" Henry said.

"All this training, all this weight-lifting and karate, it ain't gonna

THE WEIGHT LIFTERS • 137

help us one bit. Chango and his gang number close to fifty-five members. Do you think that the three of us are going to teach them a lesson?"

Henry grew red-faced, "Don't be stupid, you're always stupid! The idea is not to fight them like three crazy John Waynes. I have a plan, it deals with the philosophy of inner strength and truth. I can hurt those guys without even laying a hand on them."

Pete stepped forward, his weak eye rotating crazily in his socket, "Oh yeah? That's pretty crazy if you ask me. Those guys don't understand no philosophy, the only thing they understand is violence. And even if we did know karate, they'd take out the great equalizer." Pete made his hand into a gun, "Boom! They'd blow our brains out."

Henry grew angrier, his handsome face whitened, "You guys are so dumb it makes me sick. Sometimes I think you enjoy being pushed around by a bunch of mindless thugs. Do you really think that beating anybody up is going to solve our problems? No! We have to get to the root of the matter and I have a plan."

"What is it?" Pete exclaimed.

"You'll find out when the time comes."

Pete hesitated, he stammered, his eyes lifted upwards, "Well, well, goddamnit, it better be a good plan."

"Yeah!" Hector added, "Cause I'm tired of getting my ass kicked."

Henry smiled and threw some quick karate punches into the air, "Just trust me, men, trust me."

That night all three boys clambered into Pete's 57 Chevy painted metallic red and cruised down to Olympic Boulevard. They bought a six-pack of Miller High Life, gunned the engine, blasted the radio and whistled at all the girls over the age of thirteen. Later on they cruised down to Sunset Boulevard and honked at the freaks. On one corner, a girl donning a headful of platinum blonde hair and tight leather pants waved them down. Pete, his eyes spinning more uncontrollably than ever, stopped the car and poked his head out the window. He asked her how much she was charging and like a drill bit pumping for oil, she gestured at him with her middle finger. Laughing, they sped over to Whittier Boulevard where they competed with the other gaudy lowriders. Pete didn't have hydraulics but he was able to peel out fast enough to leave a trail of blue smoke in his wake.

Around midnight they drove back to Olvera Street. They parked the car in a darkened corner then wandered among the boutiques.

Henry was shuffling while Pete and Hector sauntered. They strolled into a store and chatted with a pretty counter girl then decided that they were hungry. After ordering beans and *arroz* in an open air restaurant, they sat under the stars to enjoy their meal. They talked loudly and boasted then all of a sudden Hector grew quiet. He was chewing on a mouthful of *arroz* when from the corner of his eye, he saw Chango smoking and leaning against a building. Nudging Henry in the ribs, he tried to talk.

"Look who's over there."

Henry glanced across the plaza. He saw Chango smoking and staring.

"It looks like the time has come." Henry said.

"What are we going to do?" Pete asked.

Henry took a long drink from his Coke then swallowed, "Kick ass."

"I thought you said we weren't gonna fight."

"Yeah." Pete added, "He probably has the rest of his gang hiding out somewhere."

Henry calmly wiped his mouth, "I said I wasn't going to fight but not everything goes according to plan. You never know, fighting might just be the only way."

Hector grew pale, "And you want us to back you up?"

Henry grinned, "You're my friends, aren't you?"

"If you say so." Pete said licking his dry lips.

Standing up, Henry left the table then started strolling across the plaza. Hector and Pete followed behind like puppies. Chango saw them coming but didn't move; the ember of his cigarette burned brightly in the night. As they walked Hector and Pete kept looking into the alleys and behind trees. When they finally reached Chango, both boys were sweating profusely.

Henry stood in front of Chango with his arms folded across his chest. He looked surprisingly calm.

"I hear, Chango, that you can't read."

Hector and Pete couldn't believe their ears.

"I also hear that your mother barely made it out of the second grade and your father can't hold down a job."

Chango stepped forward, out of the darkness, his face was scarred, his eyes were black and glistening, "What did you say, *puto*?"

THE WEIGHT LIFTERS • 139

"I said you can't read. That's why you don't have a job and you'll never make anything out of yourself."

Chango tossed the cigarette on the ground, "Who told you that?"

"Everybody knows it, man, everybody in the *barrio* can see what you are."

Chango frowned, he looked perplexed and mad, "And what am I?"

"A bum and a big fat zero."

From out of the dark ten other boys made their appearance. They were wearing woolen caps and Pendleton shirts. One boy tauntingly swirled a baseball bat.

Henry didn't falter; he stared at the other boys then glared back at Chango, "My father told me you wanted a job at his store but you didn't know how to make out the application. He said if you weren't so stupid you wouldn't have to steal everybody's lunch money."

Hector felt his heart smash against his ribs, for a moment he thought he was going to faint.

"That's why you pick on my friends. You know they have more on the ball than you do. You're jealous, the only thing you know is gang-banging, stealing, smoking dope. When they're doing good for themselves you'll still be here trying to act tough for a bunch of punks . . ."

Chango's face tightened, his tiny black eyes narrowed, "Shut-up, *puto*, before you get hurt!"

"I'm not afraid of you, Chango." Henry said, "I can read and write and if you want to find out, I can also fight."

Chango stepped forward with his fists doubled up. Henry quickly got into his karate stance. Pete trembled and Hector thought he was going to die. Henry spun around and threw a few wild kicks into the air, at the same time, he made loud, yelping noises. Then he sent out six and seven quick punches. Chango's mouth fell open, he hesitated then backed-off, wiping his nose, he asked, "Where'd you learn that?"

"From a book."

"A book?"

"Yeah."

Chango looked at Henry then at Hector and Pete; there wasn't fear in his eyes, only admiration. The gang was waiting for Chango to make a move, but Chango slowly lowered his hands. Finally, he quietly said, "Ah, leave those *putos* alone. They ain't worth fighting."

With that Chango turned around and led his gang across the

140 • David N. Monreal

plaza. Pete and Hector watched them disappear into the darkness. *Mariachi* music burst out of a restaurant door. Henry smiled, threw a few more kicks for good measure, then put his arms around his friends. They walked silently for a long time, then Hector turned to Henry and said, "What happened?"

"I scared him away."

"How?"

"Haven't I always told you dummies that truth hurts more than punches?"

Pete's eyes nearly straightened out, "Nah, you never have."

"Then you ain't been listening to me."

Laughing, they bought some Miller's and made their way back to Whittier Boulevard.

THE WEIGHT LIFTERS • 141

THE MIRACLE

Rafael C. Castillo

When Felipe saw the luminous image of La Virgen on his front door, he couldn't believe it. He felt a chill strike his bones. He wasn't religious, and he didn't go to church. So why believe now, he thought. But the image was strikingly real, and María had said it was a sign from God. He went outside and examined it again, and then asked skeptically, "Why is it that when I turn off the porch lights it disappears?"

"I don't know," she replied.

The image of La Virgen de Guadalupe had appeared to Felipe Cruz one evening when he sat on his torn Sears sofa, drinking Lone Star beer and watching an old Cheech and Chong movie. One of his neighbors who lived across the street knocked on his door and asked about the strange apparition.

"*Buenas noches, señora Gonzalez.* How can I help you?"

She was an ancient woman with a face of a prune. She blessed herself and asked Felipe to step outside. She told him that his house was blessed and that La Virgen de Guadalupe had chosen Felipe as her earthly messenger. Felipe was embarrassed and scoffed the suggestion and explained the apparition as a freak coincidence of nature. The image was created by reflected light bounced off from the chrome bumper of his souped up '55 Chevy. And when the porch lights flooded the bumper, the image of La Virgen illuminated on his front door. It was all extremely logical, Felipe explained.

The old woman was muleheaded and reiterated her claim.

"No *señor*, your house has been blessed. You must not be selfish. You must share our heavenly mother with all your neighbors."

The hefty, middle-aged unemployed artist stared at the old woman and scratched his head. His graying wisps of hair threatening to devour his balding scalp.

Meanwhile María stepped outside.

"What is it Felipe?" she asked.

Her petite figure was youthful despite their twenty-year marriage. They were without children, a lonely couple living on Guadalupe Street. She worked as a bank teller at InterFirst and supported the artistic inclinations of her Van Gogh obsessed husband.

The old lady stared at her and said, "I've been trying to make your husband understand that La Virgen has descended upon your lovely home. It's a miracle and soon everyone will know the good news."

Felipe winced, his eyes slanted. The old woman looked at Felipe and asked, "What's wrong, Pipi?"

She was affectionate with Felipe and he hated the nickname because it reminded him of his unpleasant adolescent years.

"Thank you *señora* Gonzales. Have a good day," María replied. The old woman got the message and departed. It would only be a short time before the entire neighborhood swarmed with strangers and religious franatics. And Felipe knew what headaches would descend upon him.

"Perhaps it is a sign from God," María said.

"What kind of sign?"

"That you find a real job," she smiled.

"Come off it, María. We've been through all that before. Look, we've survived with the endowment monies and that small artist-in-residence program at the ViAztlan Cultural Arts Center haven't we?"

144 • Rafael C. Castillo

María grinned and said, "Yes, but—"

"But what María."

She knew whatever she said was not about to change their relationship, but perhaps the apparition was a real sign of things to come.

The next morning, old ladies wrapped in ebony shawls and strangers appeared and requested that Felipe flip on the porch lights so they could see the reflection of la Virgen de Guadalupe. He agreed and the lights turned on. Felipe saw invalids in wheelchairs, crippled elderly people, and some not so poor. They stared at the apparition and prayed. Others fell to their knees and chanted, their arms stretched heavenward. The majority shut their eyes and clutched their rosaries, tears streaming down their wrinkled cheeks. There they prayed and prayed until Felipe asked them to leave because it was closer to morning. A week later, the crowds got bigger with more skeptics and believers.

Felipe was even asked by a stranger who wanted permission to set up his *raspa* stand on his yard. A group from the Holy Name Society wanted to sell cakes and tacos to benefit their church. Surely, Felipe was not about to refuse. But he told them No. And the groups sold their wares on the sidewalk and the street. Pretty soon, the affair with La Virgen de Guadalupe got out of control.

One week later, the parish priest visited Felipe and asked him to remove his car from the street and change the light bulb. Felipe told him he had done that last week but an angry crowd threatened him and his fence got torn down by some irate women. Nevertheless, the priest insisted. He told Felipe it was unhealthy that his parishioners stood outside every night praying to a reflection. He didn't complain when his attendance doubled since the incident.

"Well, *padre*, it's not your fault they see *La Virgen*. All I see is an image of a Lone Star longneck."

"Don't be ridiculous! Just change the bulb and leave the rest to me."

The following evening, Felipe changed the bulb and installed a yellow Bug-Lite. He even backed up his Chevy so the yellow light struck a different bumper.

More strangers arrived and more crippled people flocked to the scene. Even a CBS crew team was there. A reporter asked about the significance of the image and the neighborhood priest interjected that it was a symbol of Hope and a religious unity amongst the community. It had revived old fashioned spiritual values. The priest was cautious to add that the image was not something that was worshipped. Felipe saw from behind the window curtains. The praying got louder and then someone knocked on his door and asked that the lights be turned on.

The yellow light struck them and then the reflection hit the door. The people stared at the door. There was nothing. Not even a speck. The image was gone. The priest seized the opportunity to speak to them and asked that they visit his church. There was going to be a special mass in honor of La Virgen de Guadalupe.

Felipe was glad that the spectacle was over. Not once had he believed until his wife got home one day and told him she was expecting a child.

"But that's impossible!!!!" Juan shouted, ecstatic.

María hugged him and began crying. She confessed that she had prayed for a miracle. And now she was with child.

Months passed. The incident of La Virgen de Guadalupe was almost forgotten until the old woman from across the street got wind about Felipe and his expectant wife. That in itself was a miracle, being that Felipe and María were both in their late forties.

The child was christened Guadalupe. María had considered the name appropriate since that was all Felipe spoke about when the apparition had occurred. She was a beautiful, gentle baby.

When the old lady saw that the child had been brought home from the hospital, she paid them a visit.

"*Buenos días, señora Gonzalez,*" Felipe grinned. What's on her mind this time, Felipe wondered. The old woman gave them a basket of fruit and asked to see the new baby. She caressed the baby and then saw something strange about the child.

Felipe who had been eyeing the old woman saw her puzzled look.

"*Señora Gonzalez,* why are you staring at my daughter so strangely?"

When the old woman recognized the birthmark, she was speechless. She caught her breath, and then hollered: "María! Come quickly!!"

Felipe jumped from his sofa. María came dashing from the kitchen. When they both got closer, María and Felipe sighed and smiled and she went back into the kitchen.

Felipe relaxed and said, "Oh that. It's just a birthmark."

"Just a birthmark!!" the old woman said.

Felipe ignored her. The old woman smiled and said, "You two are

146 • Rafael C. Castillo

so blessed. It is the image of La Virgen de Guadalupe on your child's buttocks. She is going to be a special child."

Felipe winced and said, "Not again."

The old woman left immediately to spread the good news about the birth of Guadalupe.

UN DIA . . .

Margarita Tavera Rivera

Imposible hablarte, escondidio tras el periódico, la revista, el how-to-book sobre la electricidad, mis problemas, mis alegrías caen sobre oídos sordos, oídos selectivos, uh-ah, es tu respuesta frecuente a los desastres diarios, . . . ¿ y qué hicieron esta mañana? me saque el corazón, y nos lo desayunamos, con esa salsita que a ti te gusta . . . suena el periódico, hmm-que bueno, ¿y fueron a alguna parte? hicimos una excursión a Marte con paradas en Venus y en nuestra luna, ¿y compraron algo? si, encontramos unos gusanitos que bailan el can-can, y hasta medias negras traen, que bueno, los veré mas tarde, ¿y los chicos cómo se portaron? muy mal, y por eso les saque los dientes a e hice un juego de collar con unos aretes . . . ? y vieron algo interesante? . . . sí me dí cuenta que la gente arrastra sus cabezas por el cabello y que sus zapatos estan ensuelados de almas inquietas . . . me alegro ya hayan salido hoy, no es bueno que se pasen el día encerrados, . . . hay diálogos y hay monólogos y hay personas que entablan dialogosmonológicos . . . ¿sabes?, lo que tú necesitas es una mujer que te cuide la casa, alguien que puedas emplear y despedir sin problema . . . se acaban los problemas emocionales, cesan las acusaciones, . . . que tú no me quieres, que tus hijos no te importan, que nomás piensas en tu trabajo, que nada más piensas . . . el silencio crece y se hace incoportable, un silencio desordenado, la gritería de los hijos me enrrama las orejas, y pequeños zarcillos se meten en mis oídos, reclama atención, y me enfurezco, me entristezco, me aterra no poderignorarlos, no quiero que se sientan tan solos e impotentes como yo . . . estamos solos, eso lo dijiste tú, pero unos estamos mas solos que otros . . . sé independiente, y yo lo intento, pero siempre fracaso, es difícil ser independiente cuando el trabajo de una no tiene valor económico, pero quizás tú te refieras a mi independencia emocional, pero¿cómo es ese estado? ¿es qué debe uno dejar de querer a los demás? . . . pero si no los quieres como te vas a querer tu mismo; quizás la independencia emocional necesita de una independencia económica, o a lo mejor es lo contrario, tal vez se necesita un cambio . . . todo cambio mejora, al menos eso se dice, hay cambios insignifi-canes, (cambio de zapatos, cambio de camisa, cambio de vestido rojo) hay otros cambios muy importantes, (cambio de domicilio, cambio de nombre, cambio de vida) de joven los cambios pasan inadvertidos pero con el paso de los años los cambios se resienten, especialmente los cambios de compañero o compañera son los mas difíciles, . . . las personas no se pueden descartar como zapatos usados . . . que ya no nos conocemos, tenemos vidas diferentes, cada quien por su lado, cuidando su trabajo, su profesión, o su vocación, no tenemos amigos en común, los hijos ya se fueron, no queremos, o no podemos, compar-tir nuestras vacaciones, nuestros parientes se han vuelto lejanos, hay parejas que conviven solos, y les queda escasamente tiempo para cam-biar, cambiar de papel quizas . . . de hija a madre hay muchas leguas y no hay programa de entrenamiento, pero el papel de hija es on the job training, hay mas tiempo para aprenderse el role, de madre solo hay nueve meses de preparación, preparación sin práctica o es práctica sin preparación, y luego aparece un pequeño ser que espera, que exije tiempo completo, nada de que hay cuentos que escribir, ni novelas que leer, y menos tiempo para amar . . . amar se lleva tiempo, no sólo de bañarse y cepillarse los dientes, de conocerse (no en el sentido Bíblico) de saber que a él le gusta que le besen la nuca, y para ella un ramo de flores, una rosa roja son un afrodicíaco que se compara con una docena de ostiones . . . dicen que los enamorados hacen su mundo de noventa y cinco por ciento de imaginación y cinco por ciento de realidad . . . todo está en la imaginación y de allí salen las imágenes que mantienen viva la ilusión de los seres enamorados, hasta después que ya no tienen, ni el pelo sedoso, ni la piel tersa y tibia, pero que se ven asimísmos como se vieron antes, en sus tiempos de pétalos de rosa y violetas . . . ser padre tampoco es fácil, hay un desplazamiento difícil de aceptar, es un abandono físico, emocional, de la noche a la mañana deja de ser el centro de atención, ya no se le mima, muchas veces ni se atienden sus necesidades, y se pregunta, ¿quién es este intruso o intrusa que ha llegado a tomar posesión de mi tiempo, mi hogar, mi sueño, mi mujer? . . . pero el pequeño lo conquista, su manita aferrada a su dedo, la risa de caballitos, los ruidos y movimientos que hacen los recién nacidos, asi como una sinfonía, al verlo tan desvalido no puede negarle el cariño, el cuidado y la protección que necesita para sobrevivir su infancia . . . un estudio ha encontrado pruebas de que todos los bebés tienen ciertos rasgos físicos que los hace entrañables, por ejemplo, la cara redonda, la nariz chatita, los ojos grandes y redondos y la boquita de capullito, todos estos detalles en conjunto hacen del bebé un ser que despierta en los adultos un sentido de protección, este fenómeno no esta limitado a los seres humanos sino que también se ha observado en los animales . . . los gatitos, los perritos, los ositos cuando pequeños también despiertan el mismo instinto protectivo, . . . por eso es que la gente la gustan estos animales cuando son pequeños pero que al perder sus rasgos infantiles son abandonados en la calle, en el monte, algunos bebés humanos también son abandonados . . . el estudio temina citando el ejemplo del los osos pandas, que aunque son enormes, todo mundo los adora, porque, aun en su estado de adultos asemejan un osito recien nacido, y asi sobreviven . . . para sobrevivir es bueno no enfermarse, y menos en domingo, (los domingos son buenos para ir a la iglesia) enfermarse en domingo es tentar los dioses de la tecnología, ya que los doctores no trabajan los sábados ni los domingos, y lo menos posible el resto de la semana, entonces para recibir servicio médico en fin de semana es necesario ir a los hospitales, donde hay salas de emergencia, . . . las salas de emergencia nececitan una explicación, debe ser algo no muy serio, porque hay por lo menos hora y media de espera, para recibir atención debe llegar con la cabeza en la mano, o el corazón en un frasco, o en una zip-lock bag, ahora sigue los mas difícil, establecer comunicación con el personal . . . hay que hacer una confesión completa, si tiene dinero para pagar, si tiene alguien que respalde su palabra, proporcionar información sobre su situación económica, física, emocional y saber el apellido de su madre cuando soltera, ahora ya puede ocupar un sillón en la sala de espera . . . en la sala de espera, hay reuniones familiares, disgustos entre los familiares que se culpan de lo sucedido, creo que allí también se reunen los amantes que no tienen dinero para un motel, en serio . . . se dice que la medicina es una ciencia, debe de incluirse entre las ciencias ocultas, los doctores convertidos en sacerdotes, rodeados de aparatos mecánicos, y ayudantes humanos que actuan mecanicamente . . . con estos seres es difícil entablar conversación, en primer lugar por que están cansados, los trabajan demasiado, en segundo porque para ellos y ellas, es como estar en una línea de producción, abre la boca, meten el termómetro, levanta la mano, voltea el brazo, y terminado su turno te mandan con el siguiente, ahora debes desvestirte, acostarte y aguantar lo que sique . . . relájate, es difícil lograrlo tirada de espalda, desnuda en un cuarto frío, con las piernas abiertas . . . por eso es mejor estar sana y estarás a salvo un día te contaré . . . te contaré historias de hadas, cuentos de espanto, y te enseñaré unas adivinanzas, cantaremos canciones de cuna, y corridos de mujeres infieles, te hablaré de mi niñez dorada, de mi juventud penosa . . . un día hablaremos del azul del cielo, de la belleza de los pájaros y el aroma de las flores, sondearemos la profundidad del mar, lloraremos los amores perdidos, los amigos olvidados y el tiempo esfumado . . . un día rezaremos por los muertos desconocidos, los conocidos, les prenderemos veladoras a todos los santos, pero eso sera otro día.

CONTRIBUTORS

RICARDO AGUILAR MELANTZON, author of *Caravan Enlutada, En Son de Lluvia, La Poesia de Efraín Huerta,* and *Palabra Nueva: Cuentos Chicanos,* is currently a Professor of Spanish at the University of Texas, El Paso. His works have been published in *Excelsior, Journal of Ethnic Studies, La Palabra y El Hombre, Plural,* and *Revista Chicano-Riqueña,* among other publications.

ALURISTA, one of the foremost Chicano poets who has authored six collections of poetry. His work has been widely anthologized and published in a variety of journals, newspapers, and magazines.

JUAN BRUCE-NOVOA, author of *Chicano Authors: Inquiry by Interview* and *Chicano Poetry: A Response to Chaos* is presently a Professor at Trinity University in San Antonio, Texas. His critical articles have appeared in *Aztlán, Plural, Puerto del Sol, Texto Crítico,* and *Riversedge.*

RONNIE BURK, of Sinton, Texas is currently traveling throughout the U.S., and in Mexico. He is the author of *En el Jardin de los Nopales,* Mango Publications, 1978. His work has appeared in *Caracol, Maize Notebooks,* and *Revista Chicano-Riqueña.*

RAFAEL C. CASTILLO, a native of San Antonio, Texas is a writer-teacher at St. Phillip's College, in San Antonio. Publications where his work has appeared are the *Arizona Quarterly, Canto al Pueblo Anthology-Arizona, Chicano Images on Film, The English Journal, Hispanic Link, Nuestro* and *Somos.* He is the editor of *ViAztlán* and will be the guest editor for *Sahuaro Review — 1985* (University of Arizona).

ALFREDO DE LA TORRE, is a counselor and writer in San Antonio, Texas. His novel *The Lion is Out of the Cage* was awarded the National Award by Pajarito Publications in 1977 (Albuquerque, New Mexico). De la Torre has published widely throughout the U.S. in such publications as *Caracol, El Grito, New America, Nuestro, Revista Chicano-Riqueña, Revista Rio Bravo, Tonantzin,* and *ViAztlán.* He is the author of *Caracoleando,* a book of poems and *Las Dos Caras de la Migra,* a play.

ROBERTO G. FERNANDEZ, originally from Cuba, presently resides in Tallahassee, Florida. His works have appeared in various anthologies, as well as in *Nuevas Voces* (Holt & Rinehart), *Nuevos Horizontes, Linden Lane, Revista Chicano-Riqueña, Swallow's Tale,* and *Termino.* Fernandez authored *La Vida es un Special* (Miami, Ediciones Universal, 1982, and *La Montaña Rusa* (Houston, Arte Publico Press, 1985).

MAGDALENA GALLEGOS, of Denver, Colorado is a upcoming writer and graduate student in Public Administration. She is currently working on children's books and a novel.

JULIAN S. GARCIA, a resident of San Antonio, Texas is a teacher of English. He is Associate Editor of *ViAztlán.* He has published in *Caracol, Praxis, Revista Chicano-Riqueña, River City Review, Tonantzin,* the *San Antonio Light,* and *ViAztlán.* He is presently working on a manuscript, *The Mexican Jew.*

CESAR A. GONZALEZ, was born in Los Angeles, California and presently resides in San Diego. He is Chairperson of Chicano Studies at San Diego Mesa College where he sponsors, edits, and publishes *Fragmentos de Barro: Pieces of Clay,* an annual writing contest. Gonzalez has published in numerous journals, among them *Caracol, De Colores, Fragmentos de Barro: Pieces of Clay, Imagine, Maize Notebooks,* and *Palabra Nueva: Cuentos Chicanos.* His work has also been widely anthologized.

RICHARD W. KIMBALL, is a journalist whose work has appeared in various publications, among them *Gloucester Magazine,* the *Village Press,* and *Whispering Wind.* He is the author of a *A Wigwam is not a Tipi,* Tiguex Books, 1983, and *The Book of Quetzalcoatl,* presently in press. Kimball from Albuquerque, New Mexico, is a member of Western Writers of America, Inc. and the Rio Grande Writers. His writings concentrate on Native American history, culture and arts and Southwestern subjects.

DAVID NAVA MONREAL has published his short stories in *Bilingual Review, Byline Magazine, Chiricú, Firme, Maize, Revista Chicano-Riqueña, Q-VO*, and other literary journals. Monreal is of Costa Mesa, California. He has authored the book *A Pastoral Tale, Between Yesterday and Today*, and *Santa Crusing with Cooper*.

DEVON GERARDO PEÑA, grew up on the Mexican border (Laredo) and considers himself a "guerrilla researcher" (learning about the rich and powerful to inform and empower the poor.) His creative writings have been published by Aztlán, and Maize Notebooks. Peña is a Professor in the Sociology Department of The Colorado College, in Colorado Springs, Colorado. He is currently working on a new collection of poetry and prose.

MARY HELEN PONCE, of California is a widely published Chicana prose writer. She has published in *Chismearte, Fem:Revista Cultural, Maize*, the *Southern California Anthology* (USC), and *Woman of Her Word*-Arte Publico Press. *Nuestro* magazine will feature her work in the March-April 1985 issue.

MANUEL RAMOS, a native Coloradan, recently returned to creative writing after practicing law with Legal Services for ten years. A novel in progress was a finalist in the Colorado Council on the Arts and Humanities Writing Fellowship Awards for 1984.

MARGARITA TAVERA RIVERA, is presently finishing her Ph.D. in Latin American literature from Stanford University. She has written a collection of short stories, a play, and poetry, which has been published in *El Tecolote*. Margarita was born in the state of Guanajuato, Mexico and presently resides in San Antonio, Texas.

ENID SEPULVEDA, is an English instructor at Merced College, in Merced, California. Her work has been published by *Above the Hush, Apostrophe, Between the Sheets* (Cal State, Stanislaus), and *Expressions* (La Casa Agneyc, Modesta, CA). Sepúlveda was born in Puerto Rico and reared in New York's South Bronx.

FRANCISCA HERRERA TENORIO, grew up in the southwest valley of Albuquerque, New Mexico. Her work has appeared in various journals. She is presently residing in Palo Alto, California.

GLORIA VELASQUEZ TREVIÑO, is a writer from Colorado who finished her doctorate in Literature at Stanford, California and is presently teaching Chicano literature at Cal.-Poly. She is currently working on a novel.

O.J. VALDEZ is a writer from San Antonio, Texas whose focus is the confluence of two cultures from a first-hand observation post at the crossroads: San Antonio.